WINTERS' SUMMER
By
D. Lamar Jackson

Dedication

This Book is dedicated to both of my parents, Ellis and Stephanie Jackson. Mom, you were the first to tell me to write my ideas down on paper and see where it takes me. Pop, you have been my biggest supporter and I love you for it.

Chapter 1

Sean Winters

Time always seems to stop here. My world begins to make sense and all the world's troubles are gone. Here, I am where I should be. I am where I want to be. I am where I have to be. I make the rules. I have the final say. Here, I am boss, I am king, I am in control. Here, I make time stand still if only for a moment. Frame by frame, I capture what some would say is worth a thousand words. Here, I expose people for who they are. Here, I fix the world's flaws and imperfections. Here, I make the ordinary extraordinary.

Okay, I may be feeling myself just a bit much. But, if you had the life I have you would be cocky too. I mean I'm good, I'm great, I'm the best and no one can tell me otherwise. At twenty-eight years old I am on top of my game.

Better yet, I'm ahead of the game. I'm
making more money than both my
parents combined. I'm living in a nice
condo and driving this years S Class
Benz; not to mention I'm sleeping with a
model.
That's just a snapshot of my life; I'll
explain more later. Right now I have to
get on my grind and make some magic
happen. I'm an artist, digital, but an
artist still the same. I take a rough
canvas and I turn it into the photos you
see in Essence, Jet, Ebony and Hair
Magazine. I take a regular person and
turn them into what you see on club
flyers, bus benches and even billboards.
At this moment Alexis is my canvas.
At times, it's a hard job. Thank God for
photo shop Adobe. Everyone seems to
have some type of flaw I have to fix to
make them look like the people we all
strive to be. I mean I have to take out
moles, put in a mole, eradicate pimples,
widen butts, bust, hips and lips. I was
beginning to think no one was perfect
until I met this women here in front of
me. Alexis Washington, God's Mona
Lisa, His perfect canvas.
The shot is set. Miles, my assistant, has
the lights in perfect position. Melanie, a
photographer and make-up artist, works
flawlessly as usual. The set is perfect.

A white chaise lounge with purple
sheets draped over the back sits against
a green screen. A half eaten box of
chocolates sits in front of the lounge
with red roses scattered on the floor.
Alexis sits on the lounge with her legs
curved under her and a glass of red
wine in her hand. Here is my vision of
the perfect welcome home for a new
magazine B. L. A C. K.
Alexis smiles for the camera wearing
nothing but a pink tank top and
matching boy shorts. Her smile
brightens my day, like the sun when it
rises over the hills in my hometown of
Oakland, California. She is hella fine,
from her brown curly hair to her big
brown eyes and her soft brown lips
shimmering with earth tone lip-gloss.
She stands five foot ten and about a
hundred and twenty-five pounds with
perfect curves. I am her photographer.
I am her friend. I am her man. I am the
one she comes home to.
We met two years ago when she came to
my photography studio, A Moment in
Time, to get head shots. She was new to
LA and wanted to get into dancing and
modeling. I remember it like it was
yesterday. She had on little make up,
light brown lip-gloss and eye shadow. I
had been in LA for two years and had

never seen a woman that looked as good as Alexis without much make-up. She wore a silver chain around her neck with a silver cross dangling from it. It reminded me of my childhood and how far removed I was from the church and the nickname P. K., Preachers Kid.

"I'm a professional dancer," she told me when I asked what brought her in.

I almost couldn't speak to her. This had only happened to me once before. Normally I'm pretty smooth and my conversation game is seamless. But with Alexis I was speechless, even though she was like a breath of fresh air.

"My, my, name is Shh, shh, Sean." She was so beautiful that I stumbled over my words the entire shoot. She giggled at me a bit. She knew she made me a little nervous. I knew from there I didn't stand a chance. A woman wants a man with confidence and who is sure of himself. At that moment, I was like a kid in high school trying to ask a girl I liked to go with me.

"You know you should think about being a model," I told her at the end of the shoot. "I have a friend who's an agent that is looking for a girl like you." Alexis rolled her eyes. "Look, shh, shh, Sean, if you want to ask me out just ask. I am not going to be impressed by the fact you may or may not know an agent and I'm not going to jump into bed with you because I think you're going to help advance my career. Now you're a good looking guy and shouldn't be nervous about asking me out. But if you're going to start off by lying, then don't bother asking me out and just let me know how much I owe you and when I can pick up my head shots."

Her little tangent made me a little scared but at the same time turned me on. It's good to see a black woman be so sure of herself. Just like a woman needs a confident man, a man needs a confident woman. A woman who isn't confident in her self is a woman walking around with a big sign that says use me and abuse me.

I tried to regain my composure and get my swag back. "Okay Ms. Alexis, do you want to go out Friday?"

"Sorry I'm busy."

My mouth dropped; I couldn't believe she just played me. I had fallen and out of love in less than a minute.

Alexis walks towards the exit door, stops and turns around. "I am free on Saturday."

My strength was renewed and my attraction to Alexis even stronger.

What else could I say? "Saturday at seven then?"

"You have my number on the paper work I filled out." She smiles and exits. I immediately got on the phone and called my agent friend, Maria. Even though Alexis didn't believe I had a friend who was an agent, I did. We went to Cal State East Bay together where she majored in Theatre. Maria, who was my very first customer, had me do her headshots when we were still in school. She came to LA about a year before me and started working at a talent agency while looking for acting jobs. She became an agent and started sending all of her talent to me when I touched down in LA. If it wasn't for Maria, I probably wouldn't be as successful as I am now. It's because of her I am contracted with her agency and five other agencies in LA. Plus, a lot of new talent that comes to town looking for headshots are recommended to come to me.

"Hey, Maria, I have just seen a girl that you may want to work with."

"Really?" Maria says, "And since when do you refer people to me?"

"Since this firecracker just changed my life. She's a dancer but she has the look of a model without even trying."

"Okay, well if you think she's good, have her meet me on Monday morning at ten."
"I will."
I hang up the phone and pat myself on the back.
That Saturday I took Alexis out to dinner and on a walk along Santa Monica Beach. We had a good time, shared our meals, held hands and joked a lot. When I dropped her off at home, she informed me that she doesn't kiss guys on the first date. This is when I told her about Maria and her wanting to meet her on Monday. At first she didn't believe me, so I gave her the address, time and phone number to Maria's agency. After that, Alexis broke her rule of not kissing on the first date. This wouldn't be the last time we broke a rule.
Alexis met with Maria and it didn't take long before she landed her first print ad. That was two years ago and Alexis has stayed on her grind. She has been in several print ads and music videos. The last one had her away from me for a few weeks. It made me realize that I loved her. Even though I had said it after only three months of dating, I didn't really mean it until she was away. I decided to buy a ring and I have just been

waiting for the right time to give it to
her. Maybe I'll ask her this weekend
when I take her up to Oakland to visit
my parents and celebrate my father's
church anniversary.

Alexis walks over to me, her golden
brown skin shinning from the sweat and
make-up. She smiles and my heart
melts. Her big brown eyes put me in a
trance. The shoot is over and it's time
to pack up but I can't move because I
am still so mesmerized by her beauty.

"You ready to go home?" Alexis asks, in
the sweetest voice. She pulls on one of
the middle buttons of my tan shirt. I
can tell she's feeling hot. She tells me
all the time that she wants me more as
when I'm taking her picture than any
other time. Something about our photo
shoots is so sexy to her that she has to
remind herself that she's working. I
have to do the same.

"We can go in minute. You can go to the
office and change."

"How about I just put my sweat suit on
but leave what I have on for you?"

"You have some stuff at home similar."
I remind her.

Alexis feels the fabric of the underwear,
her small hands caressing her skin. "I
don't have anything this nice."

10

I look at her and smile. At this moment I'm happy. Not because Alexis is half naked, not because of the way she feels on the fabric, not because she is beautiful. I am happy because she is mine and all mine.

"I will buy you some for your birthday." She smiles and kisses me softly on the lips. Her strawberry lip-gloss tastes so sweet. Her soft tongue finds it's way into my mouth. I massage her tongue with mine as I put my hands on her hips.

"Get a room," Melanie says as she walks past us."

Alexis and I come back to reality as our moment of passion is interrupted.

Alexis smiles at me. "I'll be in the office changing." Alexis walks away from me and I can't tell which is more sexy, her walk towards me or her walk away from me. Either way I enjoy watching her walk.

I look around at Miles and Melanie who are cleaning up. "Alright guys! Good job today! Let's get cleaned up and go home."

They give half cheers and fake smiles. They're tired and have been up doing photo shoots for the past twelve hours. I've shot four girls today for three different magazines. I had to squeeze them all in today because I will be gone for the next three days visiting my parents. My crew is good though and don't mind putting in the long hours, especially if it means they'll get a three day weekend out of it.

Miles walks over to me. "Hey Sean, can I ask you a question?"

Miles is a cool dude. Fresh out of college with a bright future ahead of him. He stands about two inches shorter than me at about 6 foot and keeps his hair and beard wild and natural. He's my right hand man and an aspiring photographer in his own right.

"What's up Miles?"

"I know we're supposed to be off the next three days but I was wondering if I could use the studio this weekend?"

I look at Miles, thinking I can't believe this Negro. This light skinned, green-eyed cat really wants me to hand over the keys to my studio? I mean he's a great assistant but I've only known him for about six months. We're cool but I don't know if we're that cool just yet.

"I don't let anybody use my studio when I'm away. What are you trying to do?"

"Just trying to sharpen my skills. I'll bring my wife in and just take some shots of her."

Wife? Since when was this young kid
married? I thought he was only twenty-
two. What is he doing married already?
He must have knocked this girl up or
something. I mean that's the only
reason most folks get married nowadays
anyway, especially at that young of an
age. At twenty-two, I was jumping in
and out bed with so many different
women it was crazy. I wasn't thinking
about marriage, not until Alexis.
"When were you going to tell me you
were married?"
Miles looks as if he just put his foot in
his mouth. "I guess it just never came
up. Wasn't anything personal."
Melanie walks over, "I just found out
today when he showed me a picture. I
told him I would come in with him so
you don't have to worry.
Melanie is a beautiful thick, chocolate
sista with a good heart and great sense
of humor. I've known her since my
college days. In fact, we dated for about
two-minutes our sophomore year. She's
the only one that understood my on
again, off again relationship with
Summer Boyd, my childhood
sweetheart. All Melanie wanted was
honesty and she was honest with me. I
wasn't the only guy she dated. At first I
was cool with it, because she was sexy,

but after finding out she slept with some of the other guys she dated, I had to let that go.

We stayed friends throughout school. She stayed behind an extra year because she got pregnant and needed to take a couple of quarters off. Now before you judge, I want to make it clear; she was not a hoe, but a woman, who like me, was exploring all her options. When she got pregnant, she was actually a senior and in a committed relationship with a musician named Paul Rock. After college, they got married and moved to LA where she started working with me while he got a gig playing drums for an R&B group. Over the past two years, Paul or P. Rock as he is called has been making a name for himself by writing and producing songs for other artists in the business. I take my studio key off my key chain and hand it to Melanie. "If you're both going to be here, then I guess that's okay, but I'm not paying you guys for this time."

Miles shakes my hand. "Thanks, Sean, I appreciate it."

Melanie pats me on the shoulder, "See, there is a heart inside that bird chest of yours after all."

Miles laughs an uncomfortable laugh.

I pound my chest with a closed fist, "It hasn't been a bird chest since I was twelve."
"Delusional." Melanie laughs as she walks away.
I look Miles in the eye with all seriousness," Don't mess up my studio."
Miles looks back into my eyes, "I won't."
I walk to the front of the of the studio as my phone rings. I pull the phone from the belt clip and look at the caller ID.
It's Natalie, one of my childhood friends and an up and coming fashion designer. I answer.
"Hey Natalie, what's going on, Sis?"
"Nothing much baby boy. What's new with you?"
"Same old thing. Taking pictures of beautiful women all day."
"Getting paid to be a peeping tom? Your dream job." Natalie has always been sarcastic.
"Whatever Nat, what up?"
"Just making sure you and the model are coming to the opening of my store Saturday night. "
I shake my head. Natalie knows Alexis' name but never uses it. Being that Natalie has done several fashion shows and has worked with a number of models, she has come to the conclusion that all models are dumb or too into

themselves. Natalie doesn't know Alexis but has already pre-judged her based on her profession.

"Alexis and I will be there."

"Good, I want to meet this girl you are so crazy about."

I try to change the subject.

"Is Summer going to be there?"

Natalie takes a long breath. I knew I shouldn't have asked the question but at the same time I really wanted to know.

"Yes, she'll be there, Sean."

I feel myself getting excited and nervous at the same time. Summer Boyd, my first love, my first everything. I haven't seen Summer in about two years. The last time I saw her, I left her sitting in my condo. I wanted her to stay. She had other plans. She was about to become a pediatrician in Oakland. My photography business was growing in LA. I wanted to be with Summer more than anything; we just could never make it work. She was always meeting some new guy up in Oakland and I had a variety of women coming to my studio willing to do anything for a discount on their headshots. Summer has still always stayed on my mind and now I'm going to see her this weekend.

"Sean, I don't want you ruining this day for me okay. You and Summer broke up a long time ago; you both are dating other people so don't go bringing up the past."
Natalie was right, the past is the past but I still had feelings for Summer. We talked on the phone a few times after she left the last time. We still cared for one another, it was obvious in our conversations. What I wouldn't give to be with her one last time. To kiss her lips, to hold her in my arms, to smell her intoxicating perfume.
"I promise I won't start anything, but you better tell Summer the same."
"Boy please! You better get a clue, Summer was over you the day she left you in LA. She had a date the day she came back. Sorry baby but you're the one I'm worried about."
I'm doubly shocked. I thought Summer would have least waited a week or two before going out with a new guy. And Natalie thinks I'm the one who she needs to worry about? She must not know her friend as well as she thinks; Summer could be quite the aggressor at times. Me on the other hand, I could sleep with a girl one night and act like I don't know her the next. Even though Summer isn't the average girl, I have a

woman so Natalie need not worry about
me. On the other hand, if me and
Summer were to be alone together, who
knows what would happen?
"Look, I'll be on my best behavior,
okay?"
"You better because this day is very
important to me and I don't want to
have to beat you up. And before you
say anything just remember I beat you
up in high school and I can beat you up
now."
"Now you know that was a sucker
punch, you caught me off guard."
I remember accidentally spilling soda all
over one of Natalie's designs. I told her
to just draw another picture and the
next thing I can remember is being on
the ground and my friend Eric pulling
Natalie off of me.
"Yea, yea, just be good boy."
"I will. See you tomorrow."
I hang up the phone and walk into my
office. Alexis sits on the edge of my
mahogany wood desk.
"You ready?" She says in that soft sweet
voice of hers.
She sits there with a powder blue sweat
suit on with a pink top showing from
her half zipped sweater jacket. Her skin
still glows although the water bottle in
her hand has helped her cool off a bit.

She has a black gym bag on one of her shoulders and a small purse on the other.

"Sure we can go. Melanie can lock up." Alexis looks a little confused, "You gave Melanie a key to the studio?"

Alexis knows all about Melanie and our past and she's not jealous because she knows it was never serious. I've always been honest when in a relationship, so Alexis knows about the three different models I slept with before her and she even knows about Summer.

"I gave her my key. She and Miles are coming in to do a shoot off the clock."

"Good, because I am tired and want to get some sleep before our long drive tomorrow."

We walk out of the building and towards my sapphire blue Benz. It took a lot of hard work to get this car and I take extra special care of it. Other than my condo, it's the most important purchase I've made. It's my baby. It took almost a year before I let Alexis drive my car to a dance class one day because her car was in the shop. I called her every twenty minutes to check on the car like I was a new parent leaving my kid with the baby-sitter for the first time.

"It's only about six hours and besides you'll probably be sleep the whole time

19

anyway. There is no way I'm letting you drive."
She playfully hits me in the stomach. "What's that supposed to mean? You trying to tell me I can't drive?"
"Let's just say you drive like you live in LA."
Alexis rolls her eyes and gets in on the passenger side. I get in the driver's seat, press start and drive off.
Alexis yawns and stretches. "I am not doing this again. Teaching three dance classes then coming to do a photo shoot. I must have been out of my mind."
"We needed to get the photo shoot done this weekend. You knew we were going to be out of town for a few days."
I see her look at me from the corner of my eye. "Speaking of being out of town, is your girlfriend going to be in town this weekend?"
I pretend as if I don't know who she's talking about. "You're my girlfriend."
"You know who I'm talking about. What's her name? Oh yeah, Fall."
"Summer." I fell right into that one.
"That's right, Summer." She laughs.
In an effort to be completely open to Alexis, I told her all about Summer. I told her how Summer was my first love, my first everything. Alexis has never met Summer but knows her like her

sister. Alexis even knows how Summer and I split apart or grew apart or fell apart.

"Summer may be there; I'm not sure." I say trying not to smile.

I don't know why I lied. I knew Summer would be around and that I was going to run into her at some point. Maybe I want to protect Alexis' feelings. She's told me how she's been cheated on by every boyfriend she's ever had until me. I know she can be insecure and have a hard time trusting. I especially know she doesn't trust other women because she's been burned by some so called good friends. I try not to mention Summer around Alexis because even though they've never met, Alexis is jealous of Summer.

"Oh please. I know she's going to be there. Natalie is opening her own clothing store. Of course Summer is going to be there to support her best friend."

I just nod.

Alexis stares at me for a few moments trying to get a reaction out of me. I concentrate extra hard trying not give her one.

"So, what are you going to say to her when you see her?"

I pretend she's talking about Natalie.

"Well, I'm going to tell Natalie I'm proud
of her and wish her success in her
business."
Alexis slaps me on the arm with an open
hand. "You know that's not who I
meant, Sean."
I know now that I have to be reassuring.
I have to think of something to say that
will let Alexis know I love her and want
to be with her. "Look, if I see Summer,
I'm going to just ask her how she is and
that's that."
"And what if she tells you that she
misses you and wants you back?"
At first she was trying to get a reaction
out of me but now Alexis is letting
jealousy take over. We stop at a red
light. I look Alexis in her eyes. "I will
tell her that she's too late, I already have
a good woman."
Alexis kisses me. The light turns green
and I drive off. Alexis turns her head
towards the window and closes her eyes.
She's trying to get a little nap even
though we should be home within
twenty minutes.
I hope what I told her was sufficient
enough to put her mind at ease. But
the truth is I don't know what I would
say to Summer if she told me she
wanted me back. It's been two years
since we had been together. Two years

since I held her in my arms. Two years
since I kissed her soft, pink lips. Two
years since we made love. Two years
since I said I love you and heard her say
I love you back.
I remember the first time I saw her. It
was the end of summer in North
Oakland, on 44th and Market, the fifth
house on the block. I was a skinny
twelve-year-old kid and was just
beginning to become interested in the
opposite sex. I remember sitting on the
stairs that led to my two-story house
listening to a little hip-hop on my boom
box stereo. I heard my mom talking
about how the new neighbors were
moving into the house across the street
from us that day so I wanted to be the
first to see the new folks on the block.
I didn't know much about the couple
that lived in the house before. My
mother said the husband couldn't keep
his hands off of his wife. I remember
the police showing up at the house on
several different occasions, a few times
taking the husband away. The wife
would cry as the police car drove away
with her husband in the back seat.
Things would seem normal for a day or
two, then the husband always came
back home and within a week the police
were called again. A few months earlier

the police and ambulance came, I saw
the husband sitting in the back of the
police car as usual but this time the wife
wasn't crying for him. This time the
wife was on a stretcher being put inside
the ambulance. I never saw her or her
husband again. A few weeks later the
house was up for sale and sold quickly.
I watch as a grey Toyota sedan pulls
into the driveway. A tall light skinned
man gets out and stretches. A few
seconds later, a beige mini van pulls
into the driveway. The side doors open
and two girls get out. One is about my
age and the other a few years younger.
Their mother gets out of the driver seat
of the car and smiles at her new home.
A giant moving van pulls up and parks
on the street. Except for a few brief
moments, my eyes never leave the first
girl to hop out of the minivan.
"What up, yo?" My best friend and
neighbor Eric Reed rides up to the front
porch on his 10-speed bicycle. He
breaks my trance, my thoughts, and my
prepubescent fantasies. He wears
coveralls with one of the pant legs rolled
up. He also has on an Oakland A's cap
backwards.
"What's up, Homie?" I say without
looking at him. At least that's what I

think I said. My eyes stay locked on the girl across the street.

Eric puts the kickstand out and lets his bike rest in front of my house. He walks up and stands next to me on my red porch.

"So I see the new people is moving in. Think they know a woman got killed in there a few months ago." Eric always liked to point out the negative in every situation. I don't know why but he can never see the positive.

Natalie, another neighbor and good friend, walks up to my porch and stands on the stair above Eric, making her look a little taller. "What's up Sean and Loser?" Natalie is always so cheerful and full of life, but she will talk about you in a second.

I greet Natalie but Eric takes a step further.

"Loser! You calling me a loser and you wearing the same outfit you were wearing yesterday?"

Natalie can always be seen in a pair of blue jeans and a black top and black headband.

"Man, I don't know. If they do know, they don't look like they care. And if they don't know don't mean they need to know." I finally answer Eric's question.

"I'ma go tell them." Eric says.

Natalie slaps Eric on the back of the head, almost knocking off his coke bottle glasses. Eric rubs the back of his head. Natalie grabs Eric by the arm and turns him to face her. "Don't do that. They don't need to know about that lady getting killed in their new house."
Eric tries to justify his reasons. "Why not? I would want to know if my new house might be haunted."
I stand. "The house isn't haunted. She's fine. I mean they're fine."
Natalie pops me on the shoulder. "You like the girl over there, don't you?"
I rub my shoulder and try to hide my true feelings. "No, I don't even know her."
Eric and Natalie look at each other and I can tell that they are thinking the same thing.
Eric speaks first. "Well, lets introduce you."
Eric and Natalie start heading towards the new neighbors. I try to get them to stop but once they have their minds set on something, they do it. I finally give up and walk slowly behind them. We all look both ways before crossing the street. As we walked up the short driveway, we see the mother taking the younger girl into the house. The older girl stands at the mini van and tries to

help her father with a box. She turns to see us walking towards her and looks a little worried and scared.

"Daddy," she says in an almost whisper. Her Father stops doing what he's doing and looks at us, probably thinking who are these three hoodlums walking up his driveway.

"Are you three the welcoming committee?" He asks in a strong deep voice.

Eric is the first to blurt something out. "We just wanted to let you know that your house may be haunted because a lady got..."

Natalie covers Eric's mouth to silence him. "We were just coming over to say hello."

"Well, hello. My name is Dr. Thomas Boyd." Dr. Boyd reaches his hand out for one of us to shake it.

Eric pulls Natalie's hand from his mouth and shakes Dr. Boyd's hand.

"My name is Eric, but everybody calls me Eazy Money, because I make making money look easy."

"Nice to meet you, but I think I'll call you Eric."

Natalie shakes Dr. Boyd's hand next. "My name is Natalie, future fashion designer, and I'm the smart one in this group."

I shake Dr. Boyd's hand last but I still
have my eyes fixed on Dr. Boyd's
daughter who's giving me that shy girl
smile and keeps looking away.
"My name is Sean. I live right across
the street."
Dr. Boyd smiles and nods his head. "I
saw you on your porch checking us
out." He takes his hands and brings his
daughter close to him. "This is my
oldest daughter Summer. My youngest,
Nicole, just went into the house with her
mother."
Summer waves at us. "Hi."
Dr. Boyd takes the box from Summer.
"Why don't I help your mother inside
while you stay out here and make some
new friends."
"Okay, Daddy."
Dr. Boyd takes the box and walks into
the house. Eric walks up to Summer.
"Did you know a woman got killed here
a few months ago?"
Summer gets a little nervous and begins
to back up. Natalie slaps Eric in the
back of the head. She takes Summers
hand as Eric rubs his head.
"Don't mind him, Summer, your house
is not haunted or anything."
"You sure?"
I walk up to Summer. "We're sure. But
if you have any problems you can

always come across the street to my place and I'll protect you."
Summer looks at me. Our eyes finally lock on each other for longer than a few seconds. "You promise?"
"Cross my heart and hope to die," I say as I actually make a cross on my chest with my finger.
I smile at her. She smiles back. This was the beginning of a life-long love affair with the two of us. Well, at least a twelve-year affair. We shared a lot together over the years. Our first kiss, our first date, our first dance and even our first sexual experience. Even when we weren't together, we were always there for each other. When she left me, I didn't think I could ever love again until I met Alexis. Now, after two years, I think I'm ready to marry Alexis.
I pull into the garage of my two story Condo and park. I look over at Alexis who has been asleep the whole car ride home. She is such a good woman. I feel bad sometimes because I compare her to Summer a lot. I've compared every woman to Summer, which is probably why none of my relationships last; but I'm determined to make this one last. It's not like I'm getting any younger. Not saying twenty-eight is old, but I thought

I'd be married by now. The thing is, I
thought I'd be married to Summer.
I take my hand and run my fingers
softly through Alexis' curly brown hair.
She stirs a little. She looks so beautiful
when she's asleep. I smile at her as she
rubs her nose. She then opens her eyes
as she notices that the engine has
stopped running.
"We're home already?" She must have
really been tired if she fell into such a
deep sleep. I know the days she teaches
dance are exhausting but with the photo
shoot tonight, she's probably beyond
tired.
"Yeah, just got here."
Alexis stretches her arms and neck.
She sneezes twice into her arm trying
not spread any germs. She reaches for
the glove box. "Do you have some
tissues in here? My nose is running."
I try to stop before she opens the glove
box and finds my surprise, but I'm too
slow. Alexis is stunned and motionless
as she sees the tiny black ring box in
my glove box. She puts one hand on
her chest and the other over mouth.
She looks at me, her eyes filled with
tears, but not flowing down her cheek. I
smile at her, that's all I can do now that
the secret's out. She reaches for the box
and slowly takes it out of the glove box.

Her hands shake as she opens the box
and finds a two-karat, princess cut,
diamond engagement ring.
"Is this what I think it is?" He voice
shaky as she tries to fight back tears.
She looks at me and that's when a tear
comes down the side of her face.
" I was going to wait until this weekend
to ask you."
"Ask me what?" As if she didn't know.
"We've been together these past two
years and I feel we should take it to the
next level. So, Alexis Rene Washington,
will you marry me?"
Alexis smiles through a flowing stream
of tears. She nods and gives me a yes.
She leans over and gives me a long kiss.
She then takes the ring and slides it on
to her ring finger.
"Come on, Sean, let's go inside to
celebrate."
Alexis gets out of the car and heads for
the door that leads to the house. She
stops and looks back at me as I sit
behind the wheel of my car. She smiles
and I smile back. I can't believe I'm
engaged now and to Alexis. This wasn't
my plan. I wanted to wait until Sunday
before coming home to ask Alexis to
marry me. That would give me enough
to time to see Summer, see if there was
something still there for us. I want to

make sure it's actually over with us or if we should be together. I don't want to hurt Alexis but I know I can't marry her unless I know how Summer feels about me. Summer may have left me but I know she still loves me. But does she love me enough to get back with me? As I look at Alexis standing by the door, I'm starting to think that I have made a big mistake.

Chapter 2

Alexis Washington

I walk into the two-bedroom condo
feeling like I'm in a fairy tale. After all of
the heartache and pain I have endured
over my entire life, I'm finally happy. At
twenty-six years old I've lived a life that
some sixty-two year old women couldn't
imagine. Until I met Sean, I thought my
life was all about losing. Losing my
mother eight years ago. Losing my big
sister to a man who married and moved
her to Atlanta. Losing my little brother
to the street life and eventually to jail.
Losing boyfriend after boyfriend. Losing
job after job with no real direction.
The two things that make life worth
living for me are love for God and my
love for dancing. It was my mother who
made me go to church every Sunday
with the neighbors because she had to
work. She would read the Bible to me

every night before I went to bed and taught me that no matter what my situation, God is there protecting me, loving me and caring for me. I miss my mother more than anything but I take comfort in knowing she's in heaven with God and doesn't have to deal with the stress of life anymore.

I deal with the stress of life through dance. I first fell in love with dancing when I joined the praise team at my church in Chicago, Illinois. Whenever I did a praise dance, I felt closer to God. My love for dance then branched out when I found a dancing school near my home. My mother, always supportive, found a way for me to take the classes. I got so good that by the time I was fourteen, I was teaching two dance classes on Saturdays. I dreamed I would be able to go to Hollywood and become a famous choreographer and create dance moves for music videos and movies. Little did I know all of my dreams would come true and then some.

I toss my gym bag on the couch and walk up the stairs. I go to the washer and dryer, which is right next to the stairs and across from the master bedroom. As I take a load out of the washer and put it in the dryer I finally hear Sean walk in the door. I wonder what's going through his mind as I start the dryer and proceed to take a load of dirty clothes and put them into the washer.

I have been waiting on Sean to propose for over a year now. I knew he was a good guy from the moment we met. Even though Sean was obviously nervous around me, I could see he had a good heart. When I walked into to his studio to get head shots I had no idea I would be meeting my future husband. I was fresh out of a two-year relationship with a drug dealer named Keith who helped usher my little brother James into the life. He was physically and emotionally abusive, but he kept me in nice cars and expensive clothes. But after my brother went to jail, I saw that the life I was in wasn't for me. So, I left him and Chicago in search of a dancing career. A few weeks later my ex was arrested. My brother gave him up in order to receive a lighter sentence. Now James will be getting out next year, hopefully in time for my wedding. Keith is serving ten. James has found God and tells me that he wants to be a minister when he gets out. I'm hoping he comes to Los Angeles with me when he gets out. I don't want him in Chicago

when Keith gets out. Keith and Sean
are like night and day. Had I stayed in
Chicago, I never would have met Sean.
I remember the day I met Sean vividly. I
had been in Los Angels for a little over a
year. I was getting nowhere fast. I went
on audition after audition and couldn't
get a job because I didn't have a resume
or headshots. A girl I met at several
auditions told me where she got her
headshots done and told me the
photographer was good and fine. I
decided to go to Sean's studio, A
Moment in Time. I knew right off the
back that if Sean asked me out it
wouldn't be long before we slept with
each other. I was trying to be good. I
made the mistake of sleeping with a guy
before really knowing him and then
finding out it was a big mistake. With
Sean, I didn't want to make that same
mistake.

Sean stood about six foot and had
beautiful milk chocolate skin. I noticed
his narrow brown eyes that looked
honest. No facial hair, so I got full view
of his thick chocolate lips that begged to
be kissed. He kept licking them, which
made me think about him licking me.
He was dressed casual in a pair of dark
denim jeans with a brown button down
shirt and brown dress shoes. I was in

love with him before he even spoke. But
he almost blew it when he spoke. His
stuttering was cute and I wanted to get
to know him better. Much better.
Sean was a perfect gentleman. He was
smart, funny, and most of all good
looking. But what Sean had that all of
my past boyfriends didn't have was a
loyal spirit about him. I could tell that
no matter what, Sean wouldn't cheat on
me like all of my boyfriends in the past
have. I learned that by seeing how long
he could wait before having sex or
pressuring me to have sex. Sean never
pressured me or made it seem that he
could have any woman he wants, and
right now he wants me, so I better get
with it or miss out. Truth is, I came
close to sleeping with Sean on our first
date when I found out he got me a
meeting with an agent. But I held back
and only kissed him. For weeks I had to
fight the urge to give it up to Sean every
time we were together. It was probably
harder for me to hold back than it was
for him, or at least it seemed that way.
"Sean, you gonna take a shower?" I call
down to him. He still hadn't made his
way up the stairs.
" Yeah, I'll be up in a minute," he
replies.

I turn on the washing machine and walk
into the bedroom. I sit on the bed and
look at my ring in amazement. I still
can't believe I'm actually getting
married. The sad thing is I don't know
who to call first. I could call my sister
but the two of us have never really been
close. She's always been into herself
and in her own world. She would
always act as if the world owed her
something because she was born. I just
could never be that self-centered, not
when God is my center.

I think about my Aunt and cousins that
live in LA. Aunt Gloria, my mother's
younger sister, would be happy. I look
at the time and decide to call her in the
morning because it's pretty late and my
aunt has to be to work early in the
morning. I decide to call my cousin
Simone, who is Aunt Gloria's oldest
daughter and my former roommate
when I moved from Chicago. I take my
cell phone from my jacket pocket and
dial Simone's number.

Simone answers by the third ring.

"What's up, Cuz?"

"Guess what, Monie?"

"Girl, it is too late to be playing the
guessing game. You better spit it out or
tell it to dial tone." Simone snaps back.

"Sean finally did it." I say as Sean walks into the bedroom, taking off his shirt and showing off his toned body as he walks to the closet. The site of Sean's body makes me moist. I love that my man stays in shape. With my working out all the time to stay fit, I couldn't be with someone who didn't take the same care with their body.

"What, he proposed to you?" Simone says with a bit of sarcasm.

"Yes, Girl, I'm getting married."

Simone and I scream like little teenage girls. I go over all of the details about how I found the ring and then Sean proposing. Sean walks out of the closet, shakes his head and smiles at me. He walks to the bathroom and closes the door, which signals that he has to do number two before taking his shower. Otherwise he would leave the door open so I can get a little show while he bathed himself.

"So girl, we are going to get to planning as soon as you come back from Oakland?" Simone says with more excitement than I could have imagined. Simone is about a year younger than me and has a son, Daniel, whom I grew close to while we were sharing an apartment in NoHo. Simone helped me get used to the LA life and we have been like best friends ever since. We saw each other every once in a while when we were kids, but never really got to spend time together like we did when I came from Chicago.

"You know you're going to be my maid of honor, right?"

"You would want me to be. I would have to disown you if I wasn't," Simone says with a laugh.

"Alright, Monie, let me get off this phone and get to bed. We have a long drive tomorrow. I'll call you later though."

"Okay, love you, Cuz."

"Love you too." I say as I end the call.

I could have never imagined that I would be in a ton of print ads, choreographing musicals, teaching several dance classes and getting married to a great photographer. I've only been in LA for three years but my life has done a complete one-eighty and I am happy everyday. I just pray this joy never ends.

I get down on my knees and instead of just praying I praise God for all the wonderful things He's done in my life. I thank Him for taking me from one extreme to another. At one point in my life, I had no faith in love, but now, I believe in love. As I finish my praise, I hear the toilet flush then the shower begins to run. I pray the joy I have right now is never taken away.

As I begin to fold the clothes I took out of the dryer, I pick up a pair of boy shorts Sean bought me for his birthday last month. He says he loves to see me in them, especially when I'm just walking around the house. It makes me think if Sean had ever bought boy shorts for any other women. Has he ever bought some for Summer, his first love? I've never been insecure, but knowing that Summer will be in Oakland this weekend makes me feel uncomfortable.

I know all about Sean's past relationship with Summer. Summer seems to be the only woman who he has never gotten over. I know we will run into her this weekend at Natalie's grand opening of her store. I'm not sure how I feel about meeting Summer for the first time. I wonder how Sean will act when he sees Summer. Are old feeling going to resurface? Will he think he made a mistake by proposing to me tonight? I then begin to wonder if that's why Sean said he was planning to wait until the end of the weekend to propose to me? Does he want to have one last fling with Summer before walking down the aisle?

I look at my ring long and hard. I will give him the ring back if he cheats, but I really don't want to give it back. It's so beautiful. It's what I've always wanted. It's my ring. So Sean better keep it in his pants this weekend and forever if he wants to marry me. Summer shouldn't even be an option. The problem, however, is that Summer is an option.

Chapter 3

Sean

I hop out the shower hoping I have washed away all the negative thoughts swimming through my mind. I'm trying to get back to myself. I'm never unsure about anything. I'm always in control. But when it comes to love, I have no say. How dare love make me second-guess myself! I have been with Alexis for two years now. We have loved and have made love. There should be no doubt that I have come to the right decision. She is the one for me.
I grab my towel and dry off, while I look in the mirror and see the man I have become. Not a hypocrite like my father, The Good Reverend Winters. I've become successful and I did it all on my own. I'm bringing in anywhere from ten to fifteen thousand dollars a month

taking pictures while my father is praying hard every day that his congregation will grow again.

I'm nothing like The Good Reverend Winters; I'm a good man and would never put Alexis through what my father put my mother through. The humiliation, the embarrassment, the hurt and the pain. So I have to leave Summer in the past so that she doesn't ruin my future.

I step out of the bathroom and see Alexis sitting on the bed wearing nothing but a smile. Her body is perfect to me. Long, smooth neck, perfect C-cup breasts, toned ABS, long legs and a nice perfectly toned ass. She has a dancer's body, very slim but curvy. She stretches her arms in the air and yawns. I feel like giving her the business right now.

"It's about time, Mr. Winters. I was about to fall asleep," she says to me in a low voice of seduction. She stands and walks to me and wraps her arms around me and kisses my biceps. I grab her waist and kiss her neck. She closes her eyes and exhales. I continue to kiss her neck. It tastes salty from the sweat but sweet because it's her. She opens her eyes and looks deep into mine. We kiss, softly, exploring each others mouths, caressing each other's tongues. I get a little more aggressive with the kissing and try to back Alexis to the bed but she stops me.

Alexis breaks the kiss, then kisses me on the neck, then pats me on the chest. "Let me go and take a shower. You know I like to be clean for you."

Alexis walks into the bathroom and turns on the shower. I need to relax my mind because Summer is still haunting me. I put on my boxers and T-shirt and walk out of the room, down the stairs to the front door where our suitcases are sitting perfectly against the side of the door.

I pick up my suitcase and check to make sure everything I need is in the bag. Satisfied, I put the suitcase back and pick up my camera bag. My Nikon camera and all my equipment are in the right place. I put the bag back. At the moment, I'm satisfied. But, I know I'll check again in the morning before we leave.

I hear my cell phone ring. I walk to the living room where I have the phone on it's charger. The caller ID says Summer Boyd. I nervously answer.

"Hello."

With the sweetest, sexiest voice, she says, "Hey, honey, how are you?"

"Summer, what's up?" I say trying to sound calm, cool and collected.

"You're coming to Natalie's grand opening, right?"

"Yeah, I'll get into town tomorrow. Are you going to be there?" I already knew the answer.

"Of course. That's my girl. You bringing your model friend?"

I know she's not jealous, is she? "Yeah, I'm bringing her, why?"

Summer's tone changes. "No need for attitude, I just wanted to meet the woman who finally got your heart. I mean she does have your heart right? You are happy?"

"Yeah, she has my heart and yes I'm happy."

"Good." Summer sounds as if she has more to say but doesn't know how to say it.

"So is that all you called for after a year, to see if I'm bringing another woman home?" I'm determined to get to the bottom of her middle of the night call.

"Are you still mad at me after all this time?" She asks as if I don't have a reason to be.

Not wanting to yell or get into an argument I simply say, "I'm over it."

She sighs. "No you're not, honey, and neither am I."

"What are you talking about, Summer?"
"Look, I miss you, I miss us, how we used to be. Before we were lovers, we were friends and I don't know..." She trails off, almost like she's fighting back tears.
I hear the shower turning off upstairs and I don't want Alexis to hear me talking to Summer. "Look, why don't I call you when I get to Oakland? We can meet up and talk."
"Okay, I'll see you then. Bye, honey."
Before I can say anything she hangs up. Can't believe she called me out of the blue like that. Man she sounded so good! Just when thought I was getting her off of my mind, she calls. Is this a sign? Perhaps Summer and I should be together. But what about Alexis? She's a good woman and I love her. But I haven't been through all my ups and downs with Alexis like I've been with Summer. Alexis has only known me through the good times. Alexis doesn't know my hurts like Summer. When I met Alexis, my business was already doing good. I already had my condo. The only bad thing is that I was still driving my old car, an old Corolla. It was bunt orange with hard plastic interior and no back seat; a real beater.

I walk back upstairs and stop by my bedroom where I see Alexis applying baby oil to her long legs. She looks sexy as hell sitting on the edge of the sink, her ass placed on a dry towel. She slowly massages the oil into her still wet skin which makes her glow. My beautiful model fiancé. Summer looked this good fresh out the shower.

Damn, I'm thinking of Summer again. Here I am with this fine woman in my bathroom, naked and wanting me to give her the best of me and all I'm thinking about is Summer. I have to find a way to get Summer off of my mind. There is no way I can give Alexis what she wants if another woman is on my mind. Maybe if I just set up a time where I can meet Summer this weekend, I won't worry about it anymore.

I walk to my second bedroom, which I've turned, into an office and storage room for all my equipment. I turn on my desk lamp and sit at my mahogany desk and look at my weekend itinerary. I'm going to meet up with Eric, then go to Natalie's store. Maybe Summer will be at the store and we can talk then. No, Alexis is going to be with me, which would be awkward. If I see her at the store, I can just set up a time to meet with her. No, I have a better idea. At the top of my itinerary I write C S (Call Summer) when home.   I'll just call her when I get to the Town. I fold the itinerary and set it to the side.

I look up and see Alexis standing in the doorway still just wearing that smile. Her brown sugar skin shimmering under the hallway light. Her seven-day a week workout regimen has paid off big time. Her breasts sit up perfectly without a bra on. Her brown nipples stand at attention. She has her hands on her hips but I'm looking at her perfectly shaved kitty, which makes me smile like a kid in a candy store.

"You were supposed to be waiting in the bed for me," she says as she walks over to the desk.

"Well, you know you take hour long showers sometimes. I figured I had some time to check my schedule."

"Damn it Sean, when are you going to stop being so anal about everything?"

"When I don't have to be."

Alexis leans in front of me, her breast in my face. She turns off the desk lamp. It's dark in the room except for the light coming from the hallway. Alexis kisses me on the lips, then neck, then my ear. "You know we have to be up and out of here in just a few hours, Alexis. You sure you want to do this?" I'm hoping

she says yes but in the back of my mind I know I'm going to be exhausted if we get into it right now. It's already ten and I'm trying to leave by three in the morning so I can get around traffic. "Shut up Sean. You know you want this just as much as me."
Alexis slides the keyboard and mouse to the side and sits on the desk. I roll my chair a little closer to the desk and softly kiss her lips. Sliding my tongue in I find her pearl and begin the suction, softly, slowly, then faster and harder. She moans, softly at first. She puts one hand on my head and with the other begins to rub her nipple. She likes this more than anything and she should because I'm an expert at it. Her soft moans become louder and louder. She lets me know she's reaching her climax. The moans become words, words become cursing, and cursing becomes heavy breathing until she screams as her body shakes and shivers. I continue the suction until she begs me to stop because of the sensitivity.
I look into her eyes as she smiles. She kisses me as we both taste her sweetness. I stand and pull down my underwear. She drops to the floor and takes me in like a missile pop. I grab her hair and make her stand. I want to

be inside of her. I pick her up and sit
her back on the desk. She takes me in
her hand and slowly eases all of me into
her sacred place. I begin to slowly move
inside her walls but she looks as if she's
not enjoying it as much.
"This is getting uncomfortable," she
whispers to me.
"What do you want me to do, Sexy?"
"Take me to the bedroom."
I pull out as she puts her arms around
my neck. I wrap an arm around her
waist and pick her up. She wraps her
legs around my waist as I carry her out
of the office and down the hall to my
bedroom all while we kiss. We enter the
bedroom and I lay her down on the bed.
"Do you want me to get a condom?" I
ask, not really caring if she said yes or
no.
"No baby, just give it to me."
I think back to the scare we had six
months ago. She can sense my
uneasiness.
"We're engaged now, you're my
husband. Now shut up and give it to
me."
Telling me to shut up turned me on and
made me want to get a little more
aggressive. Before I reenter paradise I
lift her legs in the air and over her head.
My shoulders keep her from being able

to put her legs down or move. I begin to stroke longer and harder as she calls on God for help. When God doesn't intervene, she begins to let a out a curse here and there until her body shakes like an earthquake and she lets out a loud, long yes. Her legs shake and her eyes roll to the back of her head.

After a few moments she catches her breath. "Okay, baby, you're the man. I had enough," Alexis says between heavy breaths and fanning herself.

"I'm not done yet," I tell her as the sweat from our bodies make a large wet stain on top of the comforter.

"I'll finish you off, baby," Alexis says as I let her legs down.

We switch positions and I lay on my back. Alexis climbs on top of me and eases me inside of her walls. She moves slowly at first, trying to find the right rhythm. I put my hands on her ass. She takes my hands away and interlocks them with hers and she lays them on the bed next to my head. She begins to move faster and faster making it hard for me to hold on. She sits up tall and places a hand on my chest and she begins to do what I like best. I know it's about to happen so I warn her which makes her go faster and harder. Before I know it, every muscle in my body tenses up as I explode inside of her. She doesn't stop moving until my muscles relax. She kisses me, then lays on top of me.

Breathing heavy, I wrap my arms around her. "I love you Alexis."

"I love you too, Baby."

As we lay in the bed, naked to the world, I think back to six months ago. It was the first time I had run out of condoms since Alexis and I had started sleeping together the year before. We both really wanted it but our rule was no condom, no love until we're married. But we couldn't help ourselves. I was giving her a bath because she was extremely sore from a two-hour dance show with her students. Before I knew it, we were in the tub together kissing hot and heavy. She got on top of me and began doing what she's great at, moving her hips. Not thinking, I let go inside of her. For the next three weeks we were worried that she might have gotten pregnant, but we dodged a bullet.

Barely moving Alexis and I slide under the covers still holding on to each other. My mind begins to wander back to Summer. I learned a lot about sex with Summer. We tried everything together, even hurting each other on a few occasions because we didn't know what we were doing. Sex with Summer was comfortable, familiar and always adventurous. Now Alexis isn't as adventurous. But I can honestly say she is an expert at pleasing me and giving it to me the way I like it and need it. Now I'm thinking I did, indeed, make the right decision in asking Alexis to marry me. But if it's the right decision, why am I still thinking about Summer?

Chapter 4

Summer Boyd

I sit on my couch looking at a photo of
me and Sean. He took it a few months
before he moved to LA. We were so
happy. My five-foot five body stands in
front of his six-foot frame. His strong,
masculine arms are wrapped around my
waist. I remember the way he smelled
that day. I had just bought him a bottle
of Sean Jean cologne. I also bought him
the outfit he's wearing in the picture; a
charcoal Sean Jean suit with a light
blue Sean Jean dress shirt. It was his
birthday, and I needed my man to look
good for his birthday.
I smile at the two of us posing for the
picture; looking like we were the perfect
couple. I let out a sigh. Pictures.
Pictures bring back memories and
memories bring back old feelings.

Feelings of love and being loved. Being
with Sean was the only time I've ever
been truly happy. No man has ever
made me feel the way Sean did, but now
someone else gets to feel what I used to
feel. Man oh man what I used to feel.
Just thinking about it makes me warm
all over. I think back to all the fun we
had growing up. All the things we
shared over the years. All the sex we
had. It makes me smile with both lips.
I haven't smiled in months. Not since I
found out my ex-boyfriend got another
woman pregnant.
I was actually hoping Jackson was the
one for me. He was smart, educated,
good looking and I thought all mine.
But it turns out he was messing around
with a couple of different women. I
guess I was foolish to think I was the
only one. Jackson did a lot traveling for
his job as a sports agent. I thought he
was just supposed to get women for
these athletes not sleep with them
himself. Now I'm faced with starting all
over again with someone else, which
scares the hell out of and irritates me at
the same time.
It seems I've always had bad luck with
men. Every man I've dated turned out
to be a cheater, too controlling, or just
not man enough for me. The one

exception was Sean. Sean had always been there for me over the years. He was a good friend and even better lover. Oh, and that first time we had sex on prom night was magical. We must have done it four times that night and then once in the morning. Shoot, I would have done it more but I think I dried the poor boy out. But it was so good, especially by the third time when we got a little rhythm going.

I get chills and goose bumps all over my body. Thinking about sex with Sean makes me horny. It's been over three months since the last time I had sex and my battery operated friend isn't helping, at least not enough. It has been two years, eight months, twenty-one days, and eighteen hours since I felt Sean inside of me. I want him right now but he's hundreds of miles away. But he will be in town tomorrow and I definitely plan to get my groove back. So what if Sean is bringing his little girlfriend. I don't care. I will have Sean in my bed by the end of the weekend.

Sean has always been a little weak when it comes to me. All I ever did was smile at him and he would do whatever, whenever and wherever I wanted. Sean was the perfect buddy. He was loyal, respectful, good-looking, smart and

willing to drop another girl in a second if
I needed him to. Sean was the guy I
could run to for anything. If I needed a
few dollars, I would run to Sean. If I
needed a ride somewhere, I would run to
Sean. If I needed someone to talk to, I
could always call Sean. If I needed a
shoulder to cry on, I would cry on
Sean's. And if I needed to get piped,
Sean was my on call plumber.
Maybe, in a sense, I used Sean for my
benefit. It wasn't that I didn't love him.
I just never felt in love with him, at least
not until now. Maybe it's the fact that
he seems unattainable now. Maybe it's
the fact that I have finally realized that
Sean has been the one for me all along
and I just didn't know it until now.
Maybe it's because I thought Sean
would always be there no matter what.
So why shouldn't I have a little fun and
come back to him later? But now later
may be too late.
I drop the picture on the coffee table in
front of the couch and walk to the
kitchen of my two-bedroom condo and
pour a third glass of wine. I know I
should probably stop because I know
I'm going to wake up with a horrible
hangover if I keep this up. But the wine
seems to give me a bit of courage. I just
got off the phone with Sean and was

ready to tell him that I was in love with him when he rushed me off the line. Probably because of his little model girlfriend.

"I'll show her. I was around before you and I'll be around after you, little miss video tramp."

It's time to pick out the perfect outfit. One that says come and get it Daddy. One that will have Sean staring at me and no one else. I know I'm supposed to be helping my girl Natalie get her new store in order for her grand opening on Saturday so sweats and a T-shirt would be appropriate. But with Sean stopping by, I need something a little sexier. I think I have the perfect thing. I pull out a little grey dress that hugs my thighs and stops just above the knees. Now I need something else to set it off. I pull out a huge black belt and my black high heel boots. I lay the dress and belt on the bed and set the heels in front and admire my selection. Not bad if I do say so myself. Now if I'm going to wear a sexy dress, I need to feel sexy under the dress. I walk to my dresser and go to my special drawer. I pull out a black satin thong and matching bra. I lay the bra and thong next to the dress and take another sip of my wine.

"Sean is going to want to take me in the back room when he sees this outfit tomorrow."

I'm startled by the sound of my cell phone ringing. I walk into the living room hoping its Sean calling me back. I'm hoping he's calling to tell me how much he's missed me and wants me back. I set my wine down on the mahogany coffee table and pick up the phone from the cream colored love seat. I look at the caller ID and lose my excitement. It's not Sean, it's Natalie, my best friend in the world.

"Hey, Nat, what's up?"

"Just calling to make sure you were still coming by tomorrow. You know how you do sometimes."

I know she's not saying I'm a flake. "I'm not going to fake on you, I promise. I'll be there at noon."

Natalie gets loud. "Noon, you trippin. You better have your little self there by nine."

I giggle, proud that I got her. "I'm just playing with you girl. I'll be there."

"You better."

I pause for a second, trying to figure out the best way to ask this question without sounding too excited or worse, desperate. "Do you know if Sean is going to be coming by tomorrow?"

Natalie takes a few seconds to answer. "Look, Summer, I know you're looking to get laid because it's been months since you and Jackson split, but leave Sean alone this weekend."

I roll my eyes even though I know she can't see me. I try to hide my true feelings and try to make it sound like a casual question. "What are you talking about? I just wanted to know if my friend was coming by or not."

Natalie laughs. "You can't even say that over the phone and sound sincere."

"Come on now, Nat, you know how me and Sean do." She should know, I've told her every steamy detail more than once.

"I know and that's why you need to leave him alone. He's happy with his new girl. Let him be for once. This time let it not be about you and what you want. If he is truly your friend like you just said, then let him go."

Alright, now she's annoying me.

"Damn, Natalie, you act like I use Sean as my little sex toy."

"You do. The only difference is he doesn't need batteries."

"That's not true, I love Sean and he loves me."

"No, Summer, you love Sean but Sean was in love with you."

"What if I am in love with Sean?"
Natalie pauses for a few seconds. "All
I'm asking is that you don't bring any
drama this weekend. This is the
opening of my very own store and I want
it to be drama free. Can you do that for
me?"
I hold up my right hand as if Natalie can
see it. "I promise. I will not ruin your
grand opening. I'll see you tomorrow."
I hang up with Natalie and toss the
phone back on the love seat. I grab my
glass of wine and take another sip. I
walk to my bathroom and begin a bath.
While the water runs I go back to the
kitchen and refresh my wine glass. I
can't believe Natalie would try to stop
true love. By her making me promise
not go after Sean, she's in turn stopping
two people from falling in love. I walk
back to the bathroom when my bath is
warm and ready for me to get in. I take
off my clothes, bra and panties and ease
my naked body into the tub.
As I relax in my tub I think about Sean
and how he's always been there for me
over the years. I think about one of the
statements Natalie made. Have I really
used Sean for my own personal fun and
games? I always thought of Sean as the
best type of friend. I could talk him
about anything and I could get sex

whenever and however I liked. Sean always pleased my mind, soul and body like no one else. No man I have ever been with has been able to do it as good as Sean.

"Natalie doesn't know what she's talking about." I say out loud.

Me and Sean have loved each other for years and I know we are meant to be together. I guess I just never realized how much I loved Sean until now. After so many failed relationships, I have come to the realization that Sean has been the perfect guy for me all along. And he will be mine again. I just have to figure out how to get him away from the model chick. I take another sip of my wine and smile. I've just thought of the perfect idea.

"I'll put it on him one good time and he'll forget all about her."

I know Sean has never been able to resist me when it comes to sex. All I need to do is give him some and he'll be eating out of my hand among other places. I'm not going to let anything stop me, not even the model. I will get Sean back and there's nothing the video vixen is going to be able to do about it but cry. Then after all that, I will finally have what I've always wanted. A stable,

reliable man that looks good and sexes
me crazy.

Chapter 5

Sean

The drive on I-5 is always long but today it seems even longer. All I can do is think about running into Summer again. I look over to Alexis who is singing along to Michael Jackson's "The Lady in my Life". Her singing is not great but her features are amazing. Even at six in the morning, the glow of her beauty would make the sun jealous. She wears no make up, except for a little strawberry lip-gloss. Her high cheekbones make her smile enjoyable which in turn makes any pain or frustration go away. Her full chocolate brown lips mouth the words of one of MJ's best ballads. She looks at me and smiles as she sings to me, for me, about her.

If Alexis is the lady in my life, what does that make Summer? Summer is, was such a part of me that I can't help but reminisce from time to time.   It's crazy to think out of all the things Summer and I have been through we never had a formal relationship. We filled the void for each other when we were lonely and in need of affection. We shared many first experiences together because we felt safe and comfortable with each other. Through it all, we did love each other. I would do anything for Summer and I did everything for her.

 I remember the first time we kissed, it was her idea. She had been in town for a few weeks and it was getting close to the end of summer and the beginning of the school year. We were about to be in junior high and I was starting be more and more interested in girls. They were all I could think about, but I had no idea how to approach them. One day Summer and I were at the basketball court at the end of our block, across the street from my father's church. We were the only ones on the court. Natalie and Eric were both out school shopping.
"You ever kissed a girl?"
Summer's question caught me off guard and I missed my shot. She grabbed the rebound and dribbled back to the key.

She was, and I would imagine still, a good basketball player. She beat me several times.

"Yeah, I've kissed a bunch of girls." I lied. Till this day I still don't know why men feel the need to lie about how many girls they can get. In my experience growing up you get shot down more than you actually get the girl. It wasn't until I was in my twenties that I had the confidence that I have now, knowing that if I want her I can get her and if she doesn't want me then it's on to the next one.

"How many?" She asks as she takes the shot and scores.

I toss the ball back to her. "I don't know, too many to count."

"Really." She knew I was lying but wanted to play along. "So if I kissed you right now, you wouldn't be scared?" She takes another shot and scores but this time I don't grab the ball. I just look at Summer, frozen, unable to move. I couldn't believe this fine girl just said she wanted to kiss me. Okay, she said what if, but in my mind that's the same thing.

Summer walks over and grabs the ball, then walks to me with a smile on her face. "So does that mean you would be scared?"

I wanted to scream hell yeah I'd be
scared. But I couldn't; I couldn't say
anything. She tosses the ball up and
amazingly it goes into the basket and
bounces away from us. She moves
closer to me, so close I can smell the
cherry Kool-Aid on her breath.
"Don't be scared Sean, it would be my
first kiss too."
My palms got sweaty, my temperature
rose and my nerves became bad and
shaky.   I can't move but at the same
time I feel like fainting. I've thought
about kissing Summer since the day she
moved to our neighborhood. I even
practiced in the mirror a few times. She
and Natalie had become best friends
and were at my house almost everyday.
Summer always stayed a little longer
than Natalie and at times she even had
dinner with us. She also baby-sat my
little sister a few times when my parents
were out and I was hanging with Eric.
But I never thought that she would want
to kiss me.
"What are you waiting for, Sean?" She
asks in a soft voice. I couldn't believe
she was being so forward about it.
"Are you sure you want to do this?" I
ask, hoping she would say no but
praying she would say yes.

She smiles at me and gets closer. She presses her lips to mine and holds for what seemed like forever. I don't move, I just let her take the lead. She releases the kiss and smiles at me again.

"See, that wasn't so bad was it?" She says.

Summer walks back and grabs the basketball. I stood in the same place, still frozen. She takes another shot and scores. She smiles again at me, this time my lips spread and I smile the biggest smile ever.

That was our first kiss, just the beginning of many of our firsts. Crazy how things go. I thought I would be the one to initiate my first kiss but I stood there frozen.

"Sean, what are you thinking about?" Alexis asks, which ends my trip down memory lane.

"Nothing." I lie.

"So what are your parents like in person?" Alexis asks. She's only talked with my mother over the phone but she's never been back home with me. This will be their first face-to-face encounter.

I know Alexis and I have been together for two years and it's not like she didn't want to meet my parents, it just was never a good time. I rarely make it back

home and when I do it's only for a day
or two and I stay in a hotel. With my
type of business, I'm usually working
seven days a week and with Alexis doing
shows or photo shoots, she's usually
busy everyday except Sundays.
Alexis has made it a point to go to
church every Sunday. I have no
problem with Alexis going to church; it's
just not for me. The way I see it, God is
never there when you need him. He
wasn't there to stop my father from
making a mistake. He wasn't there to
give my mother strength to leave him.
Whenever I've needed God's help, He
never wanted to help me.
"Are you going to tell me about your
family, Sean?" I almost forgot Alexis
had asked me a question.
"My mother is cool. I don't understand
why she stayed with my dad for so many
years." I get a little angry at the thought
of what my father did to my mother and
our family.
My father was once a popular preacher
in the North Oakland community. He
was well respected by all of his
members. He preached the word with
such power and conviction that you
could tell God had given him a gift.
Then my father, The Good Reverend
Winters, went and had an affair with a

young woman in the church. He says it was a lapse in judgment, but I believe he just couldn't keep it in his pants. Tricia Harris was a bombshell. Five-foot six, one hundred twenty pounds and thick in all the right places. She came to the church after leaving a five-year marriage to an abusive husband. She came to my father for counseling and instead of helping her with her problem, The Good Rev took advantage of this young vulnerable woman. He told me it was a one-time thing and it might have been because Tricia disappeared afterwards. My father was able to keep it a secret for about nine months until he got a call telling him that Tricia had just given birth to a baby girl named Andrea. Tricia died in a car accident a few months after Andrea was born. The Good Rev was on the birth certificate as the father. I don't know how he was able to convince my mother, but The Good Rev brought the baby home and has been raising her along with my mother.

This is why I'm not so cool with God. He let The Good Rev, a pastor, give into the temptation of the flesh. Then He didn't give my mother strength to leave. Instead He burdened her with raising my father's child. And God still allows

my father to get up in the pulpit and
preach the word like he's never done
anything wrong. I don't get it and so I
decided that I was done being a good
Christian boy because it obviously
doesn't matter what you do, you're still
going to heaven.

"All you ever say about your pops is that
he's a hypocrite." Alexis presses the
issue.

I didn't want to talk about my father
with her. I get angry when I think about
what he put my mother through. It's
been eighteen years and my half sister
Andrea has grown to be a beautiful
woman. I don't blame her for her
parent's affair because she didn't make
them sleep together. The Good
Reverend Winters gave into temptation.
He was weak and therefore a failure to
my mother, his congregation and me.
He's supposed to be our example and
above the sins and temptations of the
world.

Andrea just graduated from Oakland
Technical High School and is trying to
figure out whether she wants to go to
college or move to LA with me and
become a professional dancer. She's
been taking dance classes for years and
she choreographs all the praise dances
at my father's church.

I look over at Alexis who is still waiting for me to tell her about my father and why I don't talk with him. I finally decide I would tell her. If she's going to marry into this family, she might as well know all the dirt.

"My father had an affair."

Alexis' mouth drops. She looks shocked and confused.

I continue. "He slept with a woman who went to our church. The woman got pregnant and got hit and killed by a drunk driver a few months later. My father took the baby in and my mother adopted her about a year later."

Alexis turns her head to the road ahead, her mouth still wide open. I'm wondering now if I should have told her anything. Would she think that was too much information or would she think my family is crazy? Would her new knowledge cause her to break off our engagement less than twenty-four hours after I put the ring on her finger? I'm wondering what's going through her mind. I hope she's not thinking of leaving me, don't know if I could handle that. Then again, it would open a window of opportunity for Summer.

Alexis finally speaks. "Wow! Your parents love must be beyond strong."

"Or my mother is just weak." I don't
know why I said that. I don't think my
mother is weak. She had to be strong to
put up with me as a teenager.
Alexis puts her hand on my thigh.
"Your mother has to be a strong woman.
Anybody who would take in a child
that's not theirs and raise it and care for
it makes them a strong person."
"I guess." I had never thought of it that
way. My mother could have left my
father, but she suffered the same
gossip, stares and humiliation he did, if
not more because now she's raising his
child.
"Do you think you would ever cheat on
me, Sean?"
It was a question I thought she would
have asked a long time ago but I guess I
had earned her trust and proved that I
was for her only. It also was a question
I was afraid to answer because what if it
did happen one day? Would that make
me a liar?
"No, I wouldn't cheat on you." This is
the best answer. Most women wouldn't
want you to say yes because that just
tells them that they need to dump you
and move on to the next man. If you
answer no, you keep the peace. The
problem is that most men don't know
what they would do if they were put in

that situation. It's hard to say no when it's right there for you to take. For men, sex is like being offered a piece gum. You're more than likely going to take it even if you've just gargled with mouth wash.

"What if you run into Summer?" Alexis asks

My hand slips on the steering wheel and the car almost goes into the other lane. I easily get it back on track but my mind is racing trying to figure out why Alexis would ask that question. I know of Alexis' insecurities. She had five boyfriends in a row all cheat on her and two of them got other women pregnant while with her. We didn't sleep together for the first six months of our relationship because she truly was trying to be celibate. She had been hurt so many times that she didn't want to jump into bed with just anyone. She had fallen in love with me as I did with her so she wanted to take our relationship to the next level and, of course, I didn't complain. I mean it was hard going six months without sex. Me and the playboy channel became real good friends. But I figured Alexis was the kind of woman worth waiting for. And she has not disappointed me once. She cooks, cleans, gives good love and

she gives me space when I need it.
She's encouraging, thoughtful, funny
and smart. She's all the things Summer
was to me, maybe more.
"Summer? What does she have to do
with this?"
She rolls her eyes. "Come on, Sean,
don't play me for an idiot."
She was right to fear the meeting
between me and Summer. I don't know
what I will do when I see her. I think
about our last night together, the love
we shared, the love we made. Summer
told me she wouldn't be making any
more trips to LA because she had met
someone new. I don't know why, but
that time really hurt me. Our
relationship had always been on again
off again. We only needed each other
when we had no one else. But I was
beginning to think maybe Summer and I
should try to be together on a full time
basis. But it turns out she had other
plans. Funny how things work out
because a few weeks later I met Alexis.
A few months later, my buddy Eric calls
and tells me that Summer had broken
up with the guy she left me for. I felt
bad for Summer, but by that time Alexis
and I had begun seeing each other on a
regular basis. I had even broken it off
with all of my other lady friends. Soon

after, Summer called to say that she would be in LA for a couple of days and wanted to know if she could stay with me. At this point Alexis had a key to my place and was staying over at least three nights a week. I told Summer I couldn't do it. She said she understood but sounded heart broken. Before she hung up she told me when I break it off with Alexis I should give her a call and she'd come visit. Needless to say, that call was never placed.

"What makes you think I want to hook up with Summer?" I want to know if she trusts me or does she really think that I would sleep with Summer when I see her.

"Well you told me you two were just friends with benefits, but you guys never officially ended your relationship."

"We are still friends." I really believe that Summer and I were and are life long friends.

"Oh, really you're friends? So, when's the last time you talked to her?"

I had to think for a second. I didn't want to tell her that Summer called last night while she was in the shower. That would just open an unnecessary can of worms. "It's been almost two years."

"You talked to Natalie yesterday, Eric three days ago. Why has it been two years since you've talked to Summer?" I just shrug my shoulders. I really couldn't answer that. I mean Summer and I used to talk to each other about everything but after she left the last time, our relationship changed. For the first time we were both in serious relationships, not the casual relationships we had been used to. I admit I was a bit jealous of her newfound love and it made me want to try to find true love myself, and that's why I got serious with Alexis. I guess I hadn't called Summer in the past two years because I was afraid if I did I wouldn't be able to fight the temptation to have her come for a visit.

Alexis looks out the passenger side window. "You still love her, don't you?" I don't want to lie to Alexis or to myself. That is a hard question to answer. Summer and I always told each other that we loved one another but I told the same thing to Natalie and she said it to Eric on several occasions. We were four friends who grew up on the same street. We were with each other through the good times and the bad times and we stayed friends, so, of course we loved each other. But I think Alexis' question is more of an in love question rather than the love you have for a fellow friend or family member. That I'm not sure of. I just know Summer is still in my thoughts.

"I don't know." It was the best and most honest answer I could give.

Alexis turns and looks at me. I can see her out of the corner of my eye. She's burning a hole in the side of my face with her glare stare. I'm not sure if she wants to hit me, curse me out, yell, or call off the engagement.

"You don't know, Sean Winters? You asked me to marry you and you don't know if you're in love with your ex? What the hell, dude?"

Alexis normally doesn't get angry. She's very good at getting her point across without yelling and screaming. It's one of the things that I love about her. Whenever we disagree on something, we have discussions and not shouting matches. But at this moment, Alexis is mad and her voice is elevated.

"I don't know, Alexis. I don't know if we ever were in love or not."

"Well you better figure it out before we go any further with this engagement."

"What's that supposed to mean?" I ask her.

"I mean you need to confront your feelings. You need to talk to Summer and find out where the two of you stand. I would much rather you find out now rather than marrying me and then regretting never finding out. I love you enough to let you go if you and Summer are meant to be."

I couldn't believe she was saying this. She's telling me to go after Summer and find out if the two of us should be together. Out of respect for Alexis, I was planning to try and keep it casual with Summer when I see her. But if Alexis is giving me free range to explore with Summer, this would mean I wouldn't have to try and sneak a meeting with her during my trip. I could just talk with her and Alexis wouldn't mind. Or is this just a trick to see what I'll say or do? I have to make sure.

"So, you're telling me that you want me to go after Summer?"

"I'm telling you to get her out of your system. But, if you can't, let me know and I'll leave."

I'm still shocked. The woman I am engaged to is telling me she wouldn't even fight for me? Damn, I would fight for her if there was another man in her life she still had feelings for.

"So what if you meet another man and you want to be with him? Are you just going to leave me and expect me to just let you go without a fight?"
She puts her hand up and shows off her engagement ring.
"I am wearing your ring, Sean, which means there is no other man out there for me. But I guess you don't feel the same because Summer may be for you."
She got me with that one. She didn't have anyone else holding a piece of her heart. It was all me. But, me, I didn't know if I still had someone else in my heart. Summer was the only woman I had been with consistently through out high school and college. Summer and I learned about our bodies together. We learned how to please each other. I know that I am in love with Alexis but I just can't stop thinking about the love I had with Summer.
We drive in silence for a while. Alexis stares at her ring, probably wondering if she is going to have to take it off or will it be there for the rest of her life. I feel bad because I can't just fix this with an "I'm sorry" or an "I love you." Alexis needs to know that my heart is fully and completely hers, but I can't tell her it is. Summer has been such a major part of my life for twelve years. I can't just

write her off. Maybe Alexis is right.
Maybe I do need to confront Summer
and discuss where we stand. But how
do I get her out of my system? A hug, a
kiss, a sexual encounter? I don't know,
but something has to be done and
quickly because I need to know if Alexis
is truly the woman I am supposed to
marry.
I try to break the silence by changing
the subject. "Did you call and confirm
our hotel reservations?"
Alexis turns and looks out the
passenger side window. I couldn't tell if
she was mad or avoiding the question.
"Alexis, did you hear me?"
Alexis turns back to me and reluctantly
tells me that she canceled our hotel
reservations. I nearly hit the roof.
Where did she expect us to stay?
"I talked with your mom yesterday and
she said we can stay with them."
"Alexis, why would you do that? You
know that me and my father don't get
along." At this point I have gone from
angry to furious. When was she
planning on telling me we didn't have a
hotel to stay in? And who gave her
permission, yes I said permission, to
talk to my mother and make
arrangements for us?

"I know you and your father don't get along. That's why I wanted us to stay with them. You need to patch things up with your father because you never know when the good Lord would decide to take him away and you can't patch things up."

"Don't give me the good Lord stuff right now, Alexis. You have no right to get into my family business."

Alexis puts her ring finger in my face again. "When you put this on my finger you gave me the right to get into all of your business including family business."

Alexis further went on to explain how she wanted me to forgive my father and move on from the hurt and pain. She told me what it was like for her to grow up without a father and having a mother who was never around. She was left with an older sister and younger brother to fend for themselves because their mother worked two jobs. She told me she dreamed of having a close family because her family was not. Her mother died at fifty-five from a heart attack. Her big sister moved to Atlanta with her boyfriend, and her little brother is in prison for selling drugs. All of these things happened before she was twenty years old. She decided to move from

Chicago to LA to become a dancer and wound up becoming a dancer, teacher, choreographer and a print model.

"You don't realize how important family is until they're not around." She finishes, while wiping tears from her eyes.

I realized how important it was to Alexis for me to try and mend my relationship with my father. I agreed to go along with staying with my parents for her but I doubt my father and I will be able to resolve all of our issues in one weekend. I don't know if I like the fact that Alexis took it upon herself to set this whole thing up. I only planned on making a quick appearance at the church anniversary ceremony on Sunday. I didn't think I would be spending the entire weekend with my parents. My mother, I didn't mind so much. But my father was the last person I wanted to spend any time with. I thought these three days would be fun. I'd introduce Alexis to my friends and my mother. Then Alexis would spend the rest of the time traveling through my old stomping grounds. Now I'm having second thoughts about this weekend because not only do I have to deal with my parents, I need to talk to Summer about

where we stand. I hope I am able to
survive it all.

Chapter 6

Sean

I park the car on the street in front of my parents house. It looks exactly the same. A two story white house with red trim on the windows and roof and red cement steps that lead to the front and back doors. I sit and stare at the house for a few moments, unable to move. I hadn't really spoken with my father since I moved to LA five yeas ago. Alexis leans over and kisses me on the cheek and turns off the engine.

"It will be okay, baby." She tries to reassure me but I knew better. She doesn't know my father like I know him. He walks around pointing out everyone else's problems but never talks about his affair. The Good Reverend Winters acts as if he does no wrong and everyone else is doing bad.

I take a deep breath and look at Alexis. I lean in and kiss her on the lips. The taste of her strawberry lip-gloss makes me a little upset. I am now realizing that because we are staying with my parents we will probably not make love the entire weekend. The walls are paper-thin and my old bed squeaks too much for us to get away with anything freaky for the next three days. That just makes me want to see Summer even more. I mean at least she has her own place so if we wanted to get down, we'd have privacy.

"You ready?" I ask her but I am really asking to myself.

She smiles at me. "Let's go."

I pop the trunk and the two of us get out of the car. I look down 44th Street and it looks quiet, too quiet for a Friday in August. There are several cars on the street but I see no children playing. No kids riding bikes or playing football in the street. I remember when I was kid, there were always kids running around. Now I guess all the kids have grown up and moved on and there are no new kids to take their place. It kind of makes me sad because 44th and Market used to be a lively street and now it's as quiet as a cemetery.

I close the car door and grab our
suitcases from the trunk. Alexis has
one of those suitcases with the wheels
and I made use of them because her bag
is extremely heavy for a three-day stay.
We walk up the driveway, past The Good
Reverend Winters and my mother's car.
We walk up the red steps to the front
door. I ring the bell, but like during
most of my childhood, the bell wasn't
working so I had to bang on the screen
door.
I could hear my mother calling from
inside. "Just a minute."
My mother's voice was welcoming and
inviting. I felt a little calmer when I
heard her. Maybe I'd spend more time
with her this weekend and less with my
father. Hopefully he would be too busy
with his church anniversary to spend
much time at home. Wishful thinking.
Knowing my father, he was ready to
meet Alexis and grill her on her choice
of careers, especially her modeling half-
naked at times. Not that she should be
ashamed, she has a beautiful body and I
know every part of it.
A few seconds past before I heard my
mother unlock the three locks on the
main door. The main door opens and
my mother then unlocks the two locks
on the screen door and opens it. I

wonder why my parents still lived in this neighborhood after so many years. When you have to put five locks on your doors and have an alarm system, something is not right with where you live. My father says it's his home, he owns it and he will die in it. I say he's crazy because he and my mother could afford to live in a nicer neighborhood where they wouldn't need three different keys to get in the house.

"My baby!" My mother shouts with glee. She opens her arms and gives me a big hug and kiss on the cheek. I look at my mother and see the years have been good to her. She is in her mid-fifties but looks as if she could be in her late thirties. She was always a health nut and was in the gym at least three days a week. She looks toned but not muscular, and I'm glad because huge muscles are not a good look on women. Her short black hair looks wet as if she just got out of the shower. She probably just got back from the gym.

She is a few inches shorter than Alexis so she has to reach up to hug her. Alexis bends down to meet her halfway. "How are you Mrs. Winters? It's so good to finally meet you in person."

My mother ushers us into the house. "Oh, Alexis, child you call me Toni."

Toni is short for Antoinette. She's
always gone by Toni. I think I was
around ten the first time I heard
someone call her Antoinette. One of
those bill collectors calling on the phone
one Saturday morning. I guess I lied
and didn't know it when I told him that
there was no Antoinette here and he had
the wrong number.
"Okay, Toni." Alexis says with a smile
while holding my mother's hand.
We are now standing in the kitchen,
which is the first room you enter when
walking into the Winters' home. My
mother must have recently upgraded
the kitchen with all new black
appliances including a new dishwasher.
The beige cabinets and drawers match
perfectly with the black table and beige
chairs. They have also put in fake
hardwood floor the same color as the
cabinets. I think to myself this looks
good but why did they decide to change
when I left? I had to deal with white
cabinets that looked grey because of
dirt. We had an old tan kitchen table
that was always falling apart. I
remember my father every few months
putting another nail or glue on the table
or one of the chairs. And the linoleum
floor had several holes from wear and
tear. I can also remember being the

dishwasher. That's why when I moved out, one of the main things I wanted in my own place was a dishwasher.

"Mom, you really have this place looking nice! When did you do all of this?"

"After you moved out. If you didn't insist on staying in a hotel every time you came to visit, you would have seen it," my mother tells me with a hurt in her voice. I know she didn't like the void between my father and me. She could never understand why I couldn't forgive The Good Reverend Winters if she could. I guess I just wasn't ready to forgive.

"Well, that's all going to change, Toni." Alexis begins. "There will be no more avoiding family time as long as I'm around."

My mother looks Alexis over and smiles. I can see she already approves. Her thumb hits Alexis ring finger. She releases Alexis hand and looks down. I can't tell whether she's happy or sad. I think she's just in shock.

"And I see you're going to be around for a while," my mother says. "When did my son put that ring on your finger because he sure didn't tell me you two were engaged?"

Alexis looks down at her finger and smiles at me. "I guess I forgot to take it off. We wanted it to be a surprise."
She forgot to take it off, yeah right. I know women well enough to know that once that ring is on their finger, it's not coming off unless they need to get it re-sized because of weight gain or weight loss.
I jumped in. "I wanted to make it a surprise, but Ms. Nosey here found the ring last night so I had no choice but to propose."
"Well, welcome to the family, Alexis." My mother hugs Alexis, then me. She is beyond happy. My mother has been hinting at me marrying Alexis for the past year. Even though she had never met her in person, she would tell me that Alexis must be marriage material because she's the longest relationship I've had. Which, to my mother, is true because she only knew Summer and I dated in high school for a few months. After high school, Summer and I became friends with benefits and my mother need not ever know that.
I walk down the long hallway to the first room, my old bedroom, to put the bags down. I am surprised to see that my room has been turned into an office with

a desk, bookshelf, computer, a couch and a couple of chairs.

"I guess you're wondering where you are going to be sleeping?" My mother says while still standing in the kitchen. I guess she wanted me to be surprised to find that nothing was the same in the house since I left.

I walk back to my mother with bags in hand. "What happened to my room?" I ask. I am a little upset. I don't really know why I'm angry. I don't live here anymore. I guess I just thought they would miss me so much that they would keep my room the same for the memories. Now I can't remember what my room looked like before.

My mother explained that The Good Reverend Winters turned my bedroom into his study a year after I moved out. She said he never had a home office and would do most of his work at the church. Even though his church was right down the street, he was tired of having to get up, get dressed and go down to the church. So when I decided to start staying in hotels when I came to visit, The Good Reverend Winters decided on a new use for my room. My mother went on to say they got rid of my old bed and anything that seemed of no value to me, like my boom box, DVD

player and television. They took my
school year books and awards and put
them in a box in the garage.

"So, we don't have any place to sleep?" I
asked still a little upset and hurt that
my parents destroyed my room without
asking. I know they didn't need my
permission, but what if I wanted to
come and get some of my old things
before they threw them away?

"Oh boy, please, I wouldn't leave my
baby out like that." My mother walks
us over to a door next to the kitchen,
which leads downstairs. My parents
had renovated the downstairs to be a
small apartment. My mother always
opened her doors to those going through
tough times. She is a social worker and
first lady of my father's church so she
was always running into people down on
their luck. As of late though, no one
had rented the downstairs area.

My mother unlocks the door and leads
us down the stairs to the small living
area. It has everything you would need
to get on your feet. There is a small
refrigerator and freezer, a little hot plate,
cabinets to store food, a card table with
four metal chairs around it, a small TV,
a sofa bed and small closet with a three-
drawer dresser. There is also a small

bathroom with only enough room for a sink, toilet and a tiny shower.

"You're going to make us stay down here?" I ask a little in shock. The place wasn't bad for someone down on their luck but I have been spoiled with my new life in LA. My photography business has bought me a comfortable lifestyle. I don't know if I can handle sleeping on a sofa bed.

"This is fine, Toni." Alexis can see the disappointment on my face but she was trying to make the best of it. One thing about Alexis is that she never got spoiled. Even though we are both able to get the things we want and need, she held on to the times when she didn't have anything and couldn't get it even if she wanted it. This isn't bad to her and it shouldn't be bad to me considering I was living here five years ago. My parents have just recently begun to have a little extra money. I grew up poor, but I never wanted to live that way again. So, to me, this is a step back.

"Well, you kids get unpacked. I'm sure you want to get out and see your friends. Eric has already called three times this morning to see if you've arrived." My mother says as she begins to walk towards the stairs.

"Hey, Mom, where's The Good Reverend Winters?" I asked, because I hadn't seen him or Andrea, but his car was in the driveway. I guess I was thinking he might be in his bedroom avoiding me. "He took Andrea to get the brakes on her car fixed and to get an oil change." My mother went back up stairs and closed the door behind her.

I set the bags on the sofa bed and began to unpack. I thought back to when I graduated high school and was headed to college. The Good Reverend took me to get my brakes fixed, the oil changed and a tune up all in the same week. I wonder if he was giving Andrea the same speech he gave me about being responsible. He didn't want me to be dependent on him for everything, especially since I decided to live in the dorms my freshman year at San Francisco State University.

"Are you mad at me?" Alexis breaks my train of thought.

"Lets see, we went from staying at the beautiful Marriot Hotel to staying in a transit home."

She throws one of her socks at me.

"Don't be a jerk. And stop acting like you're better than this. You grew up in this house."

"Yeah, but not down here." I remind her.

"Let's just make the best of it, okay."
Alexis walks over to me and wraps her
arms around my neck. She gives me a
quick peck on the cheek. She knows
I'm still upset so she's trying calm me
down with her touch.
"I just didn't want to stay here." Her
touch always works. I'm calming down
and things don't look so bad at the
moment.
She kisses me softly on my lips. "It
shouldn't matter where we stay as long
as we are together."
Yeah, but we can't be together in this
place. Alexis can be a bit of a screamer
during sex and even if we started to get
into something, I'd be worried someone
would come down stairs unannounced.
This is going to be a long weekend if I
can't have sex. I'm no sex fiend but I
was at least hoping to get something
this weekend, especially since we are
now engaged.
I hear a car pull into the driveway. I
gently break away from Alexis and walk
to a small window next to the separate
entrance to the apartment to see my
sister and father getting out of a fifteen
year old Honda Civic. I begin to go for
the door that leads into the driveway to
greet them but change my mind. I turn
back to Alexis who has gone back to

unpacking our bags. I feel nervous
about Alexis meeting my father now.
What would he think about her
modeling and the videos she's done? All
of her work has been, in my view,
tasteful, but she has been filmed and
photographed in just lingerie on several
occasions.
"Was that your father?" Alexis asks.
I reluctantly nod my head.
"Well, are we going to go up to meet
him?" She has so much excitement in
her voice it's almost annoying. It's not
like she's meeting the President or
anything. She's just meeting my
hypocrite father, The Good Reverend
Winters.
"I thought you wanted to unpack." I try
to stall the inevitable. I know it's
impossible. I can already hear my
mother talking to my father and my
sister about Alexis.
"I'm pretty much done, Sean. We only
brought a few things. It's not like we're
moving in. We're just here for three
days."
She had a point and it looked as if she
had everything out except for our
bathroom essentials: toothbrush,
toothpaste, mouthwash, floss, hair
grease and hairbrush.

"Okay, but don't say I didn't try and warn you about The Good Reverend Winters."

Alexis sucks her teeth and smiles at me. She walks over to me and takes my hand in hers. She begins to move quickly forcing me to pick up speed. We walk up the stairs and open the door that leads to the main house. We walk in and see my parents sitting at the kitchen table and my sister Andrea standing behind my mother's chair. Everyone stops talking and stares at us for a moment. Andrea smiles and quickly walks over to me and hugs me causing Alexis to release my hand. Andrea stands about five-eight, making her about two inches shorter than Alexis. Andrea also has a dancer's body, real thin but toned. She probably works out with my mother.

"Hey, Sean, how's my big bro?" Andrea was up to something. I usually don't get a big hug and a "How are you doing" from her. Normally when I come to visit it's a quick hug and a "I'm going to the mall, see you later." Andrea either wanted something from me or at eighteen she was finally maturing.

"What's going on Drea? This is my fiancé˜ Alexis."

Alexis extends her hand only to be met with a huge hug from Andrea. "I know, mom was just telling us that you were engaged."
I don't know why but it still sounds strange to hear Andrea call my mother mom when she knows that's not her biological mother. I guess since Andrea's mom died when she just an infant and my mother adopted her when she was a year old, my mother is the only mother she's ever known or will know. But I would have thought my mother would have demanded that Andrea not call her mom. When my parents told Andrea the whole story when she was twelve years old, Andrea just said my mother was the only mother she will ever know and to her that was fine. But, for me, it's still difficult to hear.
"It just happened last night." Alexis tells her with a giant smile. She has gotten even happier after the hug from Andrea.
My father stands. He's my height but a little wider. Stress over the past eighteen years has made him age at least thirty years. He has a full head of grey hair with a matching beard. He walks with a cane due to a car accident seven years ago that almost claimed his

life. You would think after almost losing my father I would find a way to forgive him for his affair but I still can't bring myself to do so.

He uses his cane to walk to us. He extends his hand to Alexis and they shake. "Nice to meet you. I've heard a lot about you."

"Yes, I'm sorry I was never able to make it up here when Sean would come to visit, but I would be away in a show or in a photo shoot."

"You model underwear don't you?" My father rudely asks.

"Daddy!" Andrea shouts.

"What kind of question is that?" I ask almost ready to fight my old man.

My mother walks over and pops him on the shoulder. "Mind your manners, Ronald."

Alexis puts her hands up to silence our anger. "It's okay everybody. I have done some print ads in lingerie and have been in a few music videos in next to nothing."

"Ya see, I didn't ask her about anything she hasn't done." The Good Reverend Winters was trying to find out what buttons he could push on Alexis but she wasn't having it.

"But you didn't ask her about her dancing or choreography." I say, trying to give Alexis more ammunition to shoot my father's rude comments down. I would love to give her a real gun so she could literary shoot him down.

"You choreograph too?" Andrea asks with extra excitement. She has dreamed of being a professional dancer and choreographer.

"Yes, I do dance and have done choreography on two stage musicals that toured the country."

"Think you can help me with this one move I can't seem to get for the church anniversary this weekend?" Andrea becomes timid, not knowing if she has put her foot in her mouth by asking for help.

The Good Reverend Winters puts his foot in his mouth for her. "She's a Hollywood dancer, she probably doesn't know how to praise dance."

My mother slaps my father on his shoulder even harder this time, almost making him lose his balance. My blood begins to boil. Alexis has only seen me angry a handful of times but she knows my boiling point. Before I can get a word out Alexis steps in.

"Reverend Winters, my love for dancing comes from me being a little girl doing praise dances in church. I can assure you that I can help Andrea with her dance without making it too Hollywood." I think I just fell in love with Alexis all over again. She just put The Good Reverend Winters in his place in the most polite but stern way possible. My mother looks at Alexis and I can tell she's impressed at her comeback to my father. Andrea looks at Alexis as if she is her hero. My father realizes that he's not going to be able to push any of Alexis' buttons so he just smiles.

"Sean, you better keep this one." He tells me this as if I'm not already engaged to her or that he has any say in who I should be with. And he definitely can't tell me what to do anymore.

"So I take it you approve of me?" Alexis asks with a smile on her face.

The Good Reverend Winters smiles, then slowly walks out of the kitchen, down the hall, towards his bedroom. He walks slowly with his head down, defeated. I feel proud that my fiancé was the first person I've seen make my father speechless. She is going to fit in well with this family.

My mother hugs Alexis. "Welcome to the family girl. We are going to get along great."

I get a text on my phone. I check and it's from Summer. She wants to know if I made it in town yet.

"I'll let you guys talk for a second. I'm going to go to the bathroom real quick." I quickly walk back downstairs, closing the door behind me. When I'm sure no one is following me or can hear me, I call Summer back.

"Hey, you get my text?" Summer says sounding sweeter than honey.

"Yeah, I'm here." I tell her trying to keep my cool. I don't want to sound too excited that we were talking.

We sit silent for a few moments, not really knowing what to say. I want to tell her I want to see her now. I want to take her to a room, rip all her clothes off and give her the business. I want to make her moan. I want to make her scream. I want to make her call out my name in three different languages. At this moment, I want her more than anything in the world.

"I'm sorry I called so late last night," she breaks our silence, "That wasn't right and I won't do it again."

"It's cool, don't trip."

"I really want to see you today."

I don't know what to say. I want to see Summer but I'm not sure how I will act when I see her. A piece of me still wants to be with Summer but the other part of me wants to leave our relationship in the past. I want to move on with Alexis but I've never totally moved on from Summer.

"I don't know about today, Baby Girl, I'm showing Alexis around." I can't believe I just slipped up and called Summer by my pet name for her. I hope she didn't notice. But if she did notice, I wonder how she feels about me calling her Baby Girl?

"Well, are you going to be going over to Natalie's store today?"

"Yeah, I was thinking of stopping by Natalie's store." I tell her. I figure if I meet Summer at Natalie's store then I wouldn't be compelled to sex her on sight.

"Okay, well I'll be there this afternoon, we can talk then." Summer sounds so anxious to meet. I wonder what she really wants to tell me in person. It can't be that serious, can it? It's not like she had my baby and never told me, right? If that were the case, Eric or Natalie would have said something. It could be that after two years she's finally ready to admit she made a mistake when she left me to be with another man right after we made love.

"You know Alexis is going to be with me? I don't know if that's a good idea." I tell her. The last thing I need is some crazy drama while I'm up here.

"Don't worry about her. You won't after we talk anyway." Summer has this sexy but sinister tone to her voice. It makes me a little nervous but turns me on at the same time.

"Alright, I'll be there this afternoon." I tell her, giving in to her request to meet, even though my fiancé will be with me. I wonder if I should tell Summer that I'm engaged. Probably not, because it may ruin any chance of finding out what's really on Summer's mind. If she knows I'm engaged she may hide how she feels and just wish me luck. I need to know if she still wants me. I need to find out if I still want her.

"Okay, Honey, I'll see you there." Summer hangs up the phone.

I stand in the little apartment and just think to myself. I wonder if I'm making a mistake in trying to see Summer. I hear Alexis up stairs laughing with my mom and sister. She's such a good person with such a good heart and I may be in route to breaking it. Alexis is a good woman but Summer is my first love, my first everything. Summer was my best friend and Alexis is my best friend. Both women are good for me but I can only allow one of them to have my heart.

I get another text message. This time it's from Eric asking when I will be at his club. I text him back that I'm on my way. I walk to the stairs and reflect for a second. I've been home for about an hour and already I've had a run in with my dad, I've gotten stuck in this makeshift apartment instead of a nice hotel, Eric is blowing up my phone like a scorned ex-lover and my first love wants to see me. "This is going to be a long weekend," I say to myself as I walk up the stairs and into the kitchen. All three ladies are sitting at the kitchen table.

"We should get going. Eric just text me." I tell Alexis.

"Okay." Alexis turns to Andrea. "When we come back, I'll show you some moves that may be able to help."

Andrea gets all excited again. "Thank you."

"Don't thank me. We're about to be sisters. I'm happy to do it." Alexis stands and walks to me.

"Well, you kids get on out of here, dinner will be ready when you get back," my mother says walking us to the front door.

Alexis and I exit the house and get into my car.

"So, you ready to call the wedding off yet?" I ask her.

"What? No way. I love your mother and your sister and I have dancing in common."

"And my father?" I ask. To me, he may be the only reason for Alexis to call of the wedding and head home.

"Your father likes to mess with people but he's harmless."

I lean in and kiss her softly. I guess if she has survived the first meeting with my family and hasn't run away, then maybe she's strong enough to become a part of this family. I start the car and head towards Eric's club. I want to make it a quick meeting with Eric because I want to make it to Natalie's store. I have missed and want to see Natalie but I really need to see Summer.

Chapter 7

Alexis

Sean decides to take me to do a little sight seeing as we drive towards his friend Eric's club.   He makes a left on 40th and Market and drives down past M. L. K. Boulevard, the Bay Area Rapid Transit station or BART and Telegraph Avenue. The streets are a mix of run down houses with brown grass and big beautiful homes with nice lawns. I see what seems to be several homeless sitting on bus benches or just on the sidewalk.   We make it to Broadway and a 76 Gas Station. Sean makes a right and we drive past Kaiser Hospital, which seems to take up several blocks. It even looks like they are doing construction across the street. He tells me there was a shopping center called the MB Mall there before the construction started.

We continue down Broadway and pass by several car dealerships. Sean tells me the strip is called Broadway Auto Row. I try to find my next car as we pass the Mercedes Benz dealership. We pass by the Paramount Theatre which is a large theatre where Sean says all of Tyler Perry and David E. Talbert plays come when they're in town. I love gospel plays and I hope to be in one soon. I would have to play a character that doesn't sing though. He tells me that there are comedy shows and concerts almost every weekend. I tell him we have to go there one day soon. We finally make it to Jack London Square. Sean turns left onto Second Street and finds a park on the street. We walk about a block and half to a small building called "After Hours." Sean tells me Eric has always been the go to guy for throwing parties and events. He also tells me that Eric is the only one of them who opted not to go to college. He got his business license and started planning parties. Sean admits he was extremely jealous of Eric while he was in college. While Sean was struggling in school and trying to save money, Eric was pulling in thousands a month. By the time Sean graduated, Eric had this club, a house, a luxury car and dozens of tailor made suits. Even with all of this, Sean says Eric never changed. He never acted as if he was better than him and he always had him on the VIP list for all his parties.

Sean and I walk into the small club and we're immediately on the dance floor; good thing the club isn't open right now. There is a small stage to the right of us. Sean says Eric lets a lot of local up and comers perform. To the right of us are several tables and chairs. Straight ahead is a large bar. Sean spots Eric sitting on a bar stool looking over some papers. He's wearing a nice navy blue suit, a black button up shirt with no tie and a pair of Prada shades. He sees us and waves us over. I take Sean's hand as he leads me to the bar.

"What's up, Family?" Eric says as he stands and greets Sean with a handshake and hug.

"Hey, Eric. I want you to meet Alexis." He brings me a little closer.

"Hello, Eric." I say with a smile and extended hand.

"Well it's about time." Eric gives me a hug. "If Sean told me you were on tour again I was going to think he was making you up."

"I'm totally real. Good to finally meet
you. Sean is always talking about you."
Eric looks Sean up and down then back
to me. "Well it must be good things
because you didn't slap me."
We all share in a laugh. I look around
again. I notice a VIP section off to the
right of the bar behind closed doors. It
also must be the way to Eric's office.
Sean did tell me all about Eric, the good
and the bad. He says Eric has always
been a true and loyal friend and has
always had his back. He goes on to say
Eric is also a pretty boy which got him
into a lot of trouble with women. He
told me he can't count all the times he
had to cover for Eric because he was
seeing three and four women at once.
He's had baseball bats swung in his
direction, almost run over by cars and
even shot at a couple of times all
because he was with Eric when one of
his girls confronted him about cheating.
Sean used to think Eric just had bad
luck but then realized Eric brought all of
that drama on himself. All that changed
when he met Krystal.
"So, where's Krystal?" Sean asks.
Krystal is Eric's longtime girlfriend.
They have been together at least five
years without Eric even mentioning
marriage as far as Sean knows. It

seems that Krystal has made Eric give up a lot of his player ways. Sean told me Krystal is college educated, strong, independent and a manager of a bank. She and Eric have been living together for the past three years and Krystal is now seven months pregnant with their first child.

"She's over at Natalie's store helping her set up," Eric tells Sean as he goes back to looking at his papers.

"So, what was so urgent that you needed me to come down here when I got to the Town?" Sean asks.

"Man, I wanted you to bring Alexis by is all. You've been keeping her under wraps, Family." Eric says, not looking up from his paperwork.

I see Sean get annoyed. I think it's cute. All of Sean's friends want to check me out to make sure he's making the right choice being with me. I didn't have that until Simone and I became close. Perhaps if I did, I wouldn't have made so many mistakes when it came to men. Sean, however, doesn't think it's cute and cops an attitude with his friend.

"You made me drive to downtown Oakland so you can meet my woman?"

"I'm flattered." I say as I grab Sean's hand. I want to make sure Sean doesn't get too upset. It's not that big of deal to me. I also don't see why Sean got upset to begin with. The only other place we have to go is to Natalie's store. It's barely afternoon so we have plenty of time to stop by and see his other friend. But then it pops in my head. Summer is more than likely going to be there and Sean wants to see her.

Eric signs the bottom page of his paperwork and stands. He's a few inches taller than Sean but about thirty pounds lighter. They are about the same complexion and both go for the clean-shaven look, though it looks like Eric is in need of a shave right now. "What did you expect? You've been dating this woman for two years and this is the first time I'm meeting her. You met Krystal on our first date."

"That's only because you double dated with me and Summer." Sean looks as if he just put his foot in his mouth.

There is a long period of silence because Sean and Eric both feel a little awkward. I have felt Sean trying hard not to mention Summer since we had the little tiff in the car on the way to Oakland. Eric, on the other hand, looks like he's not sure if Sean has ever mentioned Summer to me.

I finally break the obvious tension in the room. "Don't worry, Eric, I know all about Summer."

Eric looks at me in awe. "And you're not a little jealous or irritated she's going to be up here this weekend?"

Sean punches Eric in the arm. "Man what's wrong with you?"

"What?" Eric asks as he rubs his arm.

"You're always putting your foot in your mouth. Like that time you called that girl in school 'Lazy Boobs' because one was higher than the other," Sean says.

Even though that sounds mean, it made me laugh a little.

"I'm just saying, if I were at an event and one of Krystal's ex-boyfriends was there, then there might be a fight at said event."

"Why?" I ask. "If Krystal is with you, then she's with you, just like Sean is with me. I'm not going to fight someone over what is already mine."

I say that but I'm a little worried about Summer. I don't want to have to fight over Sean, but if Summer tries anything I may have to put hands on her and not in a Godly way. But I shouldn't be worried because Sean is with me and has put a ring on my finger.

Eric tries to counter my last remark.
"What if it was that person's before and
they want it back?"
"Alright, Eric, that's enough." Sean tells
him.
"No, I'll answer." Alexis says. "In that
case, it is up to the person I'm with
whether they want to go backwards with
their ex or move forward with me. And I
believe that we all naturally walk
forward."
Eric begins to bow to me. I laugh and
make Eric stand. He stands and looks
at Sean.
"I like her. Hold on to her." He tells
Sean.
"I plan to. We're getting married." Sean
tells him pointing towards my ring
which I hold up for Eric to see.
Eric pulls his shades down and just
stares at the ring for a second. Sean
shakes him to try and get some type of
response out of him. He turns and
looks at me but doesn't say a word. I
slowly put my hand down, my smile
turning into a frown.
"Eric, say something man." Sean says.
Eric blinks then calmly says, "I need a
drink."
Eric pushes his shades back over his
eyes and walks behind the bar and
begins to pour himself a drink. He

offers us one but we both decline. Sean
and I both sit on bar stools.
"What's wrong, E?" Sean asks.
"First Natalie goes and gets married,
now you. What's next? Summer going
to get hitched?"
Sean asks, "What about you and
Krystal? It seems only right that after
five years and a baby that you would be
thinking of marrying Krystal."
"Me and Krystal? Married? That's a big
step." He says as he finishes off his
drink.
"And living together and having a child
isn't a big step?" I ask him. To me it
just seems like he's doing it backwards.
"You're afraid of marriage aren't you?" I
ask after Eric doesn't respond.
"Now why would I be afraid?" Eric asks
pouring himself another drink.
Sean has told me Eric comes from a
broken home. His father never married
his mother, and never really lived with
them unless he didn't have anywhere
else to go. He was what the
Temptations called a rolling stone. He
was a musician and traveled all over the
country. Eric knows of four brothers
and three sisters his dad fathered. He's
met two living here in the Bay Area.
After a while, Eric's mother moved on
with another man who treated Eric as if

he were his own. But he never married Eric mother either. Sean told me he thinks this is why Eric can't commit to marriage. His biological father and the man who helped raise him never married his mother.

"I don't know why you would be scared but I can tell you are." I continued to try and make Eric face his fear.

"To me, marriage is nothing but false hope for the people involved."

I smile. "Please explain."

"The woman has hope that the man will be faithful and it's rarely the case because every man will eventually cheat. The man has false hope that his woman will always be a freak in the bed. But they do all of that freaky stuff to get you, but after the wedding all that freaky stuff becomes nasty and they don't do those kinds of things. Which in turn causes the man to go and find someone else who will be his freak."

I wondered if that's why Sean's father had an affair. Was he not being satisfied at home? I don't think I will be like that. I love pleasing Sean too much to think it's nasty. And the way Sean goes down on me, I pray, will never stop. I wouldn't call myself a freak but I like to do whatever necessary to make sure Sean is satisfied. The only things I'm totally against are threesomes and doing it in a public place. Sean has brought that up but I quickly dismissed those fantasies. With the exception of those two, Sean has told me I've fulfilled all his fantasies. I guess the public place got fulfilled in a way because we did it on a plane before.

"Did you ever think that a woman wants her man to be more romantic or more exciting in bed? Maybe the man is doing the same old thing in bed and she wants something new or she doesn't want it at all."

"Now, Alexis, that's false hope. A man doesn't change because he gets married. If he's doing the same moves before marriage, then he's going to do the same moves after marriage." Eric smiles and walks to the other side of the bar to us.

I respond by saying, "In that case, the woman needs to communicate with her man and tell him what she wants."

Eric laughs, "Communication, that's the other problem. Neither the man or woman communicates what they want so they both walk around frustrated because they feel the other person should be able to know what they want. Contrary to popular belief, men and especially women are not mind readers."

I stand. "So what you're saying is that men and women need to communicate more?"

Eric nods. "Exactly. Stop being scared to say what's on your mind."

I walk to Eric and put my hands on his shoulders. "So have you communicated to Krystal that you're afraid to get married?"

Eric looks over to Sean and sarcastically says, "I don't like her anymore."

I take that as a compliment.

Chapter 8

Sean

After leaving Eric's lounge, Alexis and I walk around Jack London Square for a few minutes. We walk past Kincaid's Restaurant and I start to think about all the times Summer and I went there to eat. It made me think about how far we had come, because you can't go to Kincaid's without spending a hundred dollars or more. Summer and I started to go to Kincaid's when we had a little money. It made me think back to our first date, before we could afford Kincaid's.

I was sixteen, had my first car and a license to drive it. It was the summer before my junior year of high school and I felt grown. All I did was run errands for my mother and drive to the movie theatre in Emeryville or to the Jack n

the Box on Telegraph Ave, but I felt like
an adult because I was driving.
I remember standing in the driveway of
our home washing my black 1989
Honda Accord. I saw Summer across
the street sitting on her porch. I
couldn't tell if she was watching me or if
she was daydreaming. All of a sudden
she got up and walked over to me.
"You want to take me out to eat?"
I couldn't tell if it was a question or a
demand. Either way I was willing. We
had moved on from the first kiss four
years prior to feeling each other up a
few times a week. We still weren't a
couple, just a couple of kids
experimenting with our bodies, which
had both changed in four years.
I had gotten a deeper voice, a little
mustache and a little grass around my
redwood. But Summer had grown a lot,
especially over this past summer. She
had grown into a b-cup. Her hips were
a little wider and her butt a little bigger.
Her former curly brown hair was now
straight and hung just below her
shoulders. Her sexy brown eyes put me
in a trance. And her soft pink lips
would open up into a smile that was
brighter than the sun. I couldn't help
but be in awe of her.

"Where you want to go?" I asked not really caring where we went as long as we were together.

Summer thought to herself for a minute. "I'm kind of in the mood for a Casper's dog."

I had to admit I was in love with Casper's Dogs. The Caspers on 51st and Telegraph was one of our hangout spots. Eric, Natalie, Summer and I would ride our bikes almost every Saturday when it wasn't raining or Eric didn't have a basketball game. It was a way to get full for cheap and feel independent from our parents. Since we all had licenses, we seem to hardly have time to go to our hangout spot together. Summer was the only one of us who didn't have a license.

"That's cool, let me just finish drying the car and I'll take you."

Summer puts her hands on her hips, "You gonna pay for me?"

I looked at her like she was crazy. "Why do I have to pay for you?" But at the same time I was thinking that I would pay for anything for her.

"Well, it's just the two of us and you're the boy so you should pay."

I scratch my head, trying to figure out if she was saying this trip to Caspers was a date. "But it's not like we're boyfriend and girlfriend." I tell her trying to figure out her angle.

Summer puts her hands into the pockets of her yellow shorts. My eyes focus on her developing breasts through her yellow, red and white stripped tank top. I thought about how soft they were and what would happen to her when I rubbed them. I start to rise and quickly try to hold my dry towel in front of me. Just thinking about Summer made me crazy. And after four years and three girlfriends, she was still the only girl to ever let me feel her up. Our relationship was special that way.

Summer breaks my train of thought. "We could be boyfriend and girlfriend."

I look at her to see if she's joking or being serious. She avoids eye contact so she must be serious. I can't believe she actually just said that. All this time I thought she just used me to experiment with. I never thought she actually wanted to be my girlfriend.

I finish drying the car and walk to her. "You always said you want to keep it as just friends who kissed sometimes."

Summer takes her hands out of pockets and folds them then shifts her weight to one leg. "Yeah, well, when you broke up with Tenese last month I thought maybe you would have thought about us. I mean since you broke up with her, we've been sneaking off to kiss even more. I even let you touch me all over."

I did just break up with Tenese after a three week relationship. I hadn't tried more with Summer because she had a guy after her. And not that I'm scary, but Summer's crush was almost six foot and one-eighty. He also played on the football and basketball teams. I really wasn't trying to be on his bad side.

"Well what about you and Chris?"

She sucks her teeth. "I told you he is not my boyfriend. He wants to be but.... Never mind, forget I said something."

Summer tries to walk away. I grab her arm and turn her to face me. I look at her. She's still the most beautiful girl I had ever seen in my life. Her big brown eyes stare into mine. I lean in and kiss her as if for the first time. It just felt different, like there was more feeling, more passion, more love.

Summer looks at me and smiles. "So does this mean you're paying?"

I smile and kiss her again, this time just a peck. "Come on, let's go eat."

That was the summer we made it official. We were boyfriend and girlfriend, but by the time school started in September, we had broken up. She started dating Chris and I was getting girls numbers left and right. The only problem was that none of them stuck because I wanted to be with Summer. But she stayed with Chris all of Junior year and most of Senior year. I don't know what it is about the jocks but they always seem to get the finest girls in school. I didn't do so bad but being a photographer wasn't considered as tough as playing football. But the girls did love for me to take their pictures. Thinking back to that summer, that was the only time Summer and I actually called each other boyfriend and girlfriend, but it was definitely not the last time we were intimate. We didn't even have sex during that time. She always said she was saving herself for marriage. But like Eric always said, every girl is saving herself until you get her to the bedroom. I just never wanted to pressure her. After we broke up, I never thought I would have sex with Summer. I would have regretted never sleeping with her.

"Are you alright?" Alexis breaks my daydream.

"Yeah I'm fine." I try to assure her, hoping she couldn't tell I was thinking of another woman.

Alexis takes my hand as we continue to walk towards my car. "What's on your mind, Sean?"

"Just thinking about the past. Growing up here. Feels weird to be visiting Oakland when I still consider it my home." This wasn't a lie. All of my childhood memories are in Oakland. And my best childhood memories included Summer.

Alexis stops walking and looks at me. "Do you want to move back here?"

I shake my head no. "Our work is in LA," I know I wouldn't be making as much money here in Oakland as I would in Los Angeles.

"You left a lot of things here in Oakland."

I can tell Alexis means Summer. She's thinking that Summer is the one thing I'm missing in my life. I have to let Alexis know I love her and I do want to marry her. I don't want to make her feel insecure.

"But I found the best things in LA," I tell her in all seriousness.

Alexis kisses me. She takes my hand and we continue walking. "So tell me all about you growing up here."

Chapter 9

Sean

We get back to the car and drive to
Emeryville where Natalie is setting up
her new store in the Bay Street
Shopping Center, an outside strip mall.
I tell Alexis how back in day the biggest
attraction to Emeryville was the Public
Market, which was a short distance
from where the Bay Street Shopping
Center is. You can buy food from
almost every culture on earth at the
Public Market. In just over ten or so
years, more stores have popped up and
have made the once quiet town of
Emeryville a busy consumer town. I
used to think of Emeryville as just an
extension of Oakland, but it's proving to
be a thriving town in it's own right.
I park in the huge parking garage on the
third level, put the alarm on my car and

take Alexis by the hand. She
intertwines her soft smooth fingers with
mine. Just her touch makes me feel
nervous and excited at the same time.
I'm totally in love with Alexis. But I still
can't stop thinking about Summer.
Knowing the friendship Natalie and
Summer have, Summer is probably in
the store helping Natalie set up. I know
I told Summer I would meet her here
this afternoon but now I'm thinking that
it may be a bad idea.
Alexis has just shown me she is still
insecure about Summer. I wonder if
once she sees Summer would she then
think Summer is better looking,
smarter, or sexier than she is. Not that
Alexis has anything to worry about, I
mean, she is a model and her body is
beyond sexy.
I begin to get a little anxious as Alexis
and I walk down the street towards
Natalie's store. I get hot. My hands
start sweating. I start feeling sick to my
stomach. Alexis must see the
nervousness on my face. Either that or
she can just tell I'm not feeling right.
"You okay, Sean?"
I stop and look at her but can't speak.
"What's wrong, Baby?" She puts her
hand on my head trying to see if I have
a temperature.

I close my eyes and think about
Summer. When I walk into the store
and see her, what's going to happen?
Will it be awkward? Will she run to me
and kiss me and tell me how much she
misses me and still loves me? Will she
tell me she was sorry for not fighting
harder to make our relationship work
and that I'm the only man for her? Will
she tell me to dump Alexis and marry
her?
"Sean!"
Alexis interrupts my near nervous
breakdown.
"I'm good." I lie. I lie to protect her
feelings, I think. Maybe I lied to keep
my true feelings from coming out?
Alexis takes both my hands in hers and
looks me in the eye.
"I know. Don't feel nervous."
What does she mean she knows? Does
she know about the phone calls from
Summer? I know the walls are thin at
my parents place but I tried to talk as
low as possible. Does she know
Summer and I set up a meeting today?
I close my eyes again trying to block all
of these crazy thoughts that are
swarming through my mind. I open my
eyes and look at Alexis and smile. She
kisses me on the lips and I feel my
anxiety rush out of my body. I nod, put

my arm around her and we walk down a few stores until we get to Natalie's Boutique. I'm ready to take on what ever comes my way. It's finally time to confront Summer and my feelings. I look at the store and the first thing I notice is the black paper covering the inside of the windows so you can't see in. On the outside of the windows are two huge signs that say "Grand Opening Saturday at 3 PM." I try to open the door but it's locked. I knock three times, hard. A few seconds later I hear the keys rattle and the door is unlocked and opened. Alexis and I walk in, and the young lady who opened the door closes it and locks it back with her key. I look around the small boutique. It has bright vivid colors on the walls, which makes me feel at peace. The smell of incense fills the air. I look to the left where Natalie has an assortment of classy evening gowns and dresses, some on the racks while others were on well placed all black mannequins. To the right of the store are more casual wear, jeans and T-shirts . Towards the back of the store are several rows of shoes ranging from high heels, to boots, to tennis shoes and everything in between. In the center of the store are small glass cases with hand made jewelry. Next to the glass case are two wooden stands with cash registers on them. Behind one of the cash registers stands Natalie. Natalie is and has always been a beautiful black sista. Her deep dark skin looks smooth and flawless. She wears jeans that hug her hips and thighs and make her ass look picture perfect. Her white top shows her double d cleavage. A white and pink A's baseball cap covers her short black hair and hides her small brown eyes.

"I knew that was you. Where have you been? I've been waiting on you for 2 hours."

The young lady who opened the door walks to Natalie and gives her the key. She then walks to the back of the store to arrange some of the shoes.

Alexis and I walk to the register where Natalie greets me with a hug and kiss on the cheek.

"You went over to see Eric first, didn't you?"

I nod. Natalie shakes her head at me. Natalie and I were friends on the block first. For about two years, we were the only kids on the block. Then when Eric moved to 44th Street, things changed. Eric and Natalie were constantly getting into arguments and they just seemed to not like each other at all. They still seem to argue about the dumbest things even to this day. But they always have each other's back no matter what. They're like brother and sister. The same goes for me and Natalie, although we never seem to argue. Truth be told, she scared me a little. I saw her put Eric in a headlock once when we were kids and he complained of pain for two weeks.

"So this is Alexis, the model and dancer I've heard so much about?"

Alexis extends her hand. Natalie moves the hand and gives Alexis a huge hug. She's always been big on hugs and I have to admit you felt warm after getting a hug from Natalie. You also always wanted to stay on Natalie's good side because just as good as it felt to get a hug from Natalie, it felt just as bad to feel her wrath.

"You finally get to meet her." I tell her, happy to see that Alexis is doing great with my family and friends. They all seem to like her at first glance. She doesn't need to say a word, they just love her.

Natalie releases the hug and looks at Alexis and smiles. She then looks at me.

"Those magazines and video's don't do you justice girl. You're much prettier in person," Natalie turns to me, "She actually looks like she's too good for you."

We all laugh.

"I think we're just right for each other." Alexis says as she interlocks her arm with mine.

"Aww, Sean you got the girl brain washed."

We all laugh again.

I look around for a few seconds to see if Summer is here. I don't see her. My eyes lock on Natalie and she rolls her eyes. Natalie then looks at Alexis.

"So, Alexis, I know this is short notice but since you're a model and I am doing a fashion show for my opening tomorrow night, would you be willing to model a dress or two?" Natalie asks.

I answer before Alexis can. "Nat, she's a print model not a runway model, and plus she's here visiting not working."

Alexis takes her arm from mine and puts her hands on her hips. "What are you saying? I can't make it on the cat walk?"

Alexis does a model strut like she's been doing it for years. I had never actually seen her do that. The way she moved her hips made me think about how she moves them in bed. I begin to get a little aroused. She is so sexy and at times I can't believe she's all mine. I try to keep my arousal at bay so I try to think of other things. But the only other thing I can think of is Summer.

Alexis makes her way back to me and Natalie. Natalie gives Alexis a hi-five. Alexis looks at me as if to say what do think about that Mr. Winters. I think I want to see you do that tonight when we're alone.

"Well then I guess it's settled. Alexis will be modeling." Natalie doesn't need Alexis to say yes or no, the walk Alexis just did was all the answer Natalie needed. "Come on, girl, let me show you the dresses I want you to wear."

Alexis gives me a peck on the cheek and follows Natalie to the back. I watch her walk away and think of how great her ass looks in those jeans. I walk around the store for a few seconds just looking at the different clothes my friend has designed. I stop at a dress. It's not just any dress, it's the same dress Summer wore when we went to prom.

"Look familiar." A sexy voice says from behind me. I don't need to turn around to know it's Summer.

"Yeah, it's the dress you wore the first time we..."

Summer turns me around. I'm speechless. She looks better than I can

135

remember. She cut her brown hair to just above her shoulders. Her b-cup has grown into a c-cup and she's carrying a little something extra in her backside. I'm intoxicated with her perfume. It feels like I'm on a love high. Summer stands in front of me wearing a short grey dress with a huge black belt and black boots.

"Don't say that out loud." She says with a giggle.

Her sexy brown eyes make me follow her every word. I want to kiss her pink lips which are glazed with lip-gloss.

"But yes, that is the dress Natalie made ten years ago for prom. A few updates but that's the one."

"It still looks good. You still look good." I wrap my arms around her and she hugs me back for what seems like forever. I am in love with the way she smells, the way she looks and the way she feels at this moment.

Summer breaks the hug. "Thanks, Honey, you still look good yourself."

"How you been?" I ask trying to see if Alexis is coming my way while wondering if Alexis and Summer had just crossed paths.

"I've been good." She says in a sexy voice. I can smell the watermelon gum coming off of her breath. I inhale it as if it's the sweetest smell.

She brushes her hair behind her ear and lets her hand rest on her neck. She looks at me and smiles and I know I'm in trouble. Not because I have done something wrong but because I'm ready to do something wrong.

"So, I don't see your girlfriend, did you come alone?" She asks with bit of hope in her tone.

"She went to the back with Natalie. She's trying on some clothes that Nat wants her to model for tomorrow night." I can see disappointment on her face. Summer wanted me to tell her yes I left Alexis at home so that we can have some alone time. But that wasn't the case. If Summer had something to say, she needs to say it right now or forever hold her peace. And everything I have to say needs to be said right now. There's no backing down now. We're here and we need to have closure.

"I must have missed her. I was just using the rest room."

I want us to get everything off of our chest before Alexis comes back so I press the issue. "So what did you need to talk to me about?"

She sucks her teeth and puts her hands on her hips obviously annoyed that I seem to be rushing her. "Look, Sean, I just wanted to tell you that I've been thinking about you, us a lot lately." Okay, here it goes. She's about to let all of her feelings out. I have to stay strong and not give in to the temptation. But I don't think I can. If Summer asks me to come back to her place, then Alexis is going to have to find a way to my parent's place or to the nearest airport. I don't think I'm strong enough to say no to Summer. I have to keep telling myself to stay strong.

"Hey Sean." I hear a familiar voice calling out my name. I look to the side and see Krystal coming from the back of the store.

Krystal, Eric's girlfriend waddles towards us. She's about seven months pregnant and is glowing. I don't know why but pregnant women are beautiful. Maybe it's because of the new life that they are carrying inside them. Krystal looks good in her white sweats and pink maternity shirt. I smile because she has a giant bag of potato chips in her hand. I give her a big hug. "Hey, Krystal. How are you?"

"I'm good. I'm ready to drop this baby."

"You're looking good," Summer says, a little ticked off because Krystal interrupted our conversation.

"Thanks, Summer. I don't feel it though." Krystal turns her attention to me. "Now that girl you're about to marry, she looks good."

Summer rolls her eyes. I try to say something but she just walks away to the back of the store and begins talking to the girl that opened the door for us. Now I'm the one mad. I can't believe Krystal just blurted out that I'm engaged in front of Summer. That was not the way I wanted her to find out.

"So you met Alexis?"

"Oh, yeah and she's a ten. You always did have some good looking women." Krystal says as she devours another chip.

"So you and Eric getting married anytime soon?" I know that was a cheap shot, but she did just mess up a chance with Summer, if I had a chance. I guess now I'll never know.

Krystal looks at me with disgust. "You know your boy is never going to put a ring on my finger. I've been waiting five years and all he's done is get me pregnant."

"Now after five years, how does he get you pregnant?" I ask, wondering if she was like a bunch of other women I've met. They get pregnant in hopes the

139

father of the child will settle down and
marry them.

"What you trying to say, Sean? You
think I trapped him?" She's getting a
little irritated at me. Good. She
shouldn't have opened her mouth about
my engagement.

"I'm just asking?" I tell her with a smirk
on my face. A piece of me wanted her to
admit that she got pregnant on purpose.

"Well, how did you and Summer sleep
together for so long and you not get her
pregnant? Or Alexis, you've been with
her for two years and you haven't got
her pregnant."

What she didn't realize was Summer
had gotten pregnant once but we never
told anybody. She had an abortion
before anyone could notice. We never
spoke of it. It didn't stop us from
sleeping together. It just made us
become more careful.

"I just thought you guys were always
careful. I mean you're the one that
always said marriage before baby."

"Let's just say, things happen, Sean."
Krystal says still snacking on her chips.
Alexis and Natalie come from the back
room where I assume Natalie has her
office and possibly dressing rooms since
I don't see any out in the store. The two

are talking and laughing like they have been friends for years.

"Sean, Alexis is too funny." Natalie says as they make it to me and Krystal.

"No she's the funny one. She was telling me about the time she had to beat you up." Alexis says trying to hold in her laughter.

I try to defend myself. "She didn't beat me up. She just hit me and I didn't hit her back."

"That's not the story Eric told me." Krystal says sucking the crumbs and grease from the chips off of her fingers.

"Now you know the only reason you didn't hit me back was because you couldn't get up." Natalie holds her stomach. "He was like, I can't breath, I can't breath."

They all start laughing.

I start to get a little embarrassed. How is Alexis going to look at me now, knowing that Natalie once punched me in the stomach so hard she knocked the wind out of me? Eric talked about me for a month after that happened. I mean, it was my fault; I shouldn't have been joking about her hair. But in all honesty, on that day, her hair looked like she had just been through a tornado.

Alexis sees I'm getting a little frustrated.
She walks over and puts her arms
around me. "It's okay, Baby, you got
rock hard ABS now. You could take a
punch." Alexis says as she pats my
abdomen.
"Don't try and pump up his ego."
Natalie says, "He knows he's never been
a fighter."
Alexis kisses me on the cheek. "I know
you can protect me, Baby."
Now I'm feeling like I have to do
something to show my masculinity.
Like maybe Picking Krystal's pregnant
self up. Or trying to bench-press Alexis.
I know Alexis just said she knows I'm
strong now but a piece of her is always
going to remember that I was beat up by
a girl before. I've tried to forget that
incident ever since I was thirteen.
It was a hot summer day in July. I had
just got my first camera the week before
on my birthday. I was using Summer
and Eric as models. I had set up
different poses in my parents driveway
and on our red cement steps. The shots
were coming out great. Then here
comes Natalie.
I was just finishing a pose of Eric and
Summer standing back to back on the
steps. Natalie walks up and we all start
laughing. Her hair was everywhere. Of

course she didn't know what the big deal was at first.

"What y'all doing? What's so funny?"

Of course Eric points out the obvious.

"Girl, your hair looks like somebody just tried to use a vacuum cleaner on it."

We all start laughing again. Natalie, a little embarrassed puts her hand to her hair.

Sweet Summer tries to help. "It's not that bad. "

Of course I had to open my mouth and say, "Don't lie to her Summer."

Natalie pushes me. "Leave me alone before I hurt you."

"Don't mess with her, Sean, you see what she did to her hair. Who knows what she'll do to you." Eric says trying hard not to laugh. He failed.

"Whatever four eyes." Natalie turns her attention to me. "Why you didn't tell me you were taking pictures? I want to be in some."

I didn't want to say it, it just came out. "You can be in the pictures after you go and get your hair done."

Next thing I know Natalie punches me hard in the stomach and knocks me to the ground. Luckily I didn't drop the camera but I did drop any self-respect I had. I couldn't breathe; I tried gasping for air but couldn't get it. I look up and

Eric and Summer are no longer
laughing at Natalie but with Natalie at
me. That was probably the most
embarrassing moment of my life. Now
I'm standing here with my fiancé feeling
even more embarrassed. Luckily Krystal
changes the subject.

"Hey, Nat, you need me for anything
else, cause I need to get over to the club
and help Eric."

"You're good, Krystal. Go help that slow
boy. Lord knows he needs it." Natalie
tells her.

Krystal extends her clean hand to
Alexis. "It was nice meeting you."

Alexis hugs Krystal instead. "Nice
meeting you too."

Krystal and Natalie walk to the front
door where Natalie unlocks the door and
lets Krystal out, then closes and locks
the door behind her.

Alexis whispers in my ear. "Your friends
are really nice."

"That's only because you don't know
them that well." I joke.

I know my friends are cool. I just hate I
don't get to see or talk to them as much
anymore. We are all so busy nowadays
and with me living in LA, it's impossible
for us all to be around each other at
once. I still talk to Eric and Natalie at
least once a week but it's not the same.

We use to see each other everyday, now the only time I see them is when I have business here in the Bay and even that doesn't always happen.
Natalie walks back to us. "So what do you guys think about the store?"
I give Natalie a hug and tell her I'm proud of her. When I release the hug I see Summer coming our way. I look over at Alexis who sees what I see. Natalie turns around as Summer makes it to us. It feels extremely awkward. I'm not sure what's about to happen. A piece of me wants to see Summer and Alexis fight. Two women fighting over me would be sexy as hell. But in my world that doesn't happen.
Summer extends her hand to Alexis. "Hi, you must be Alexis."
Alexis shakes Summer's hand. "Yes and you must be Summer."
Summer nods as they release the handshake. "I just wanted to come over and congratulate you and Sean on your engagement."
Alexis smiles and walks to me. "Thank you. It just happened yesterday and we're excited."
Summer looks at me and sees the worried look on my face. "I can tell."
For the first time I'm looking at the two women who have a piece of my heart

trying to figure out who has the bigger
piece. For the first time I am not
comparing Alexis to Summer but rather
Summer to Alexis. Summer at the
moment almost seems fake. It's like
she's putting on a show, acting like
she's happy for me when really she
wants me back. I'm not sure if I want
her back at this moment.
Alexis, in a polite way is marking her
territory. She has every right to do so.
She is wearing my ring. But I can also
tell Alexis is showing some insecurities.
She's looking Summer up and down to
see what I loved about her. Summer
doesn't have the legs that Alexis has and
Summer is about five inches shorter
although her heels give her some height.
Summer is a little thicker in the right
places and Summer has prettier eyes.
I see Summer looking at Alexis trying to
check out the competition. Trying to
figure out why after so many years and
so many women, Alexis is the one that
stopped our friends with benefits
relationship. Summer sees Alexis as the
woman who stole her one reliable lover.
Summer has dealt with men who
cheated on her, beat on her, and used
her. But me, I would never do that to
her and I think she realized it too late.

I'm stuck speechless. I don't know what to say. Alexis has already given me permission to talk to Summer and see where we stand. But now that Summer knows I'm engaged, I doubt she would be willing to put her feelings on the line in fear of getting hurt for no reason. But I need to know what's on her mind. Why did she call me last night? Why did she want to talk to me so bad? Why does she miss me? Does she want me back? These are questions I need answered before I can fully commit to Alexis.

Natalie tries to break the tension. "Summer did you finish making sure everything was arranged properly?"

Summer takes a second to respond. She finally looks at Natalie. "Yes, Nat, everything is perfect for tomorrow."

"Good. And you have the dresses you'll be modeling tomorrow?" Natalie asks Summer.

"Yes."

Alexis speaks up. "You're modeling too? Natalie just asked me to model for her tomorrow as well."

Summer gives Alexis a fake smile. "See you tomorrow, then." Summer winks in our direction and walks away.

Natalie looks at me and gives me a motherly look. I know what it means.

She's telling me not to ruin her grand
opening tomorrow. I don't want to ruin
it and maybe she should be telling
Summer the same thing. After all, she
called me and wanted to talk.
I look at Alexis who looks at me. I can
tell what's on her mind as well. It's the
same thing on my mind. The wink
Summer just gave, was that for her or
was it for me?

Chapter 10

Summer

I slam my hand down on the bathroom sink. "Damn."
I can't believe he's engaged. This changes everything. Sean must really love this girl if he put that rock on her finger. I've gotten bigger rings from men wanting to wife me but they didn't really love me. They just wanted a trophy wife on their arm and felt that the big ring guaranteed I would be there no matter what. Even if they slept around or beat me. Or both.
"What am I supposed to do now?"
I'm trying to fight back tears. It's hard because I feel my heart breaking. The one man I love and want to be with is getting married. And Alexis seems like a good woman. Maybe Sean is gone for good. Maybe Alexis got what I was too

blind to see or too slow to get. But I should be the one marrying Sean.

I think back to five years ago when I found out I was pregnant. I had just gone through a bad break up and Sean comforted me. I flew to LA to be with him and we made love for an entire weekend. I didn't make him go buy condoms. I just wanted to feel him inside me. A few weeks later, I found out I was pregnant and it was his. He seemed like he wanted to keep it but I didn't want to mess up my chances at finishing medical school. He reluctantly wired me some money and I got the abortion. I haven't regretted that decision until now. Knowing the man Sean is, had I kept the baby he, would have married me and Alexis would have never come into the picture.

"I can't lose Sean. Maybe if we do have time to talk alone, he'll see he still loves me and drop Alexis."

I had so many things I wanted to say to Sean but didn't have the opportunity. Krystal just had to come over and interrupt with her pregnant ass. She stopped me from telling Sean that I love him and have always loved him. I needed to apologize for not seeing it sooner. I wanted to tell him I made a mistake leaving him for another man. I only did it because I knew if things didn't work out I could always come back to him. But that wasn't the case. Sean never complained when I met someone new and wanted to be monogamous with that person. Hell it always seemed as if he had a girl or two waiting in the wings. But whenever I broke up with a guy and went back to Sean, he would always drop those other girls quick and just be with me. That is, until Alexis.

I was really hoping Alexis would be unattractive. Of course I had seen Alexis in some magazines and music video's, but with the right make-up team you can make anyone look sexy on camera. But even with the little make-up Alexis was wearing today, she looked beautiful. And, Alexis seems to be what I failed to be, loyal to Sean.

I have to face the fact that Sean may be gone from me forever. Time to go back out to the store and help Natalie finish setting up. I adjust my dress and make sure my make-up still looks good. I don't want to walk back out to Natalie's store looking sad or depressed. I open the bathroom door and head to the front area of the store. I barely take two steps before Natalie comes out of nowhere and grabs me by the arm.

"Nat, what the hell?"

Natalie leads me into her small office and closes the door. She releases the hold she has on my arm and just stares at me for what seems like forever. I rub my arm all while wondering what was Natalie's problem. She had no right to grab me the way she did and drag me in here like I was her child. I want to push or slap her but I know better, Natalie would have whooped my ass in two point five seconds.

"Don't think I didn't see that wink." Natalie finally says, looking like a mother about to chastise her child.

"You trippin, Nat."

"I told you to let Sean be. He's got a good woman. Don't mess it up for him."

I just smile at her. I don't want her to see the hurt in my eyes. "All I did was congratulate him on his engagement."

Natalie folds her arms. "Don't nobody believe that fake congratulations."

"Whatever." I roll my eyes and try to head for the door but Natalie blocks my path. "Come on, Nat, let me out."

"Summer, I'm telling you to let it go. Please."

I look at my best friend and wonder why she isn't on my side right now. Why doesn't Natalie want me to fight for Sean? Doesn't she believe in true love?

Natalie is the one who is married. And
she married Charles after fighting her
feelings for another man. Now she's
happy and all because she didn't give up
on her one true love.
"Natalie, I love him. Can't you see
that?"
"I love Sean too, but I'm not in love with
him, and I don't think you are either."
I'm shocked by Natalie's statement.
How would she know if I was in love
with Sean or not? She doesn't know my
heart like I do. I know now that I've
been in love with Sean since high
school. I just never accepted it. Now
that I'm older and have had some bad
relationships, I know Sean is the man
for me. Sean would never cheat on me.
He would never use or abuse me. He
would never break my heart.
"I am in love with Sean."
Natalie shakes her head. "You're not in
love with him. You're just horny and
he's your safety net."
There's a knock on the door. The door
opens and in walks Charles, Natalie's
husband. He's the total opposite of
what you would expect Natalie to end up
with. He's about an inch shorter than
her, very thin and he's a computer geek.
He makes pretty good money, doing IT
work for Kaiser Permanente's home

office in Downtown Oakland. And from
what Natalie says, he's a beast in bed.
He's also one of the few guys I know that
isn't scared of Natalie.

"Hey, sorry for interrupting, I got off
work early and wanted to see if you
needed some help setting up."

Natalie walks to her husband and gives
him a kiss. "We're pretty much
finished, but, if you want, you can go
get us a table at the Elephant Bar and
I'll be there in a few minutes."

"Sounds good." Charles and Natalie
kiss again, with more passion. Charles
exits the office closing the door behind
him.

Natalie turns around with a huge smile
on her face like she's on cloud nine. It
disgusts me at the moment. Why does
she get to be happy and I don't? I
deserve a good man like her. Sean is
that good man and right now Natalie is
blocking. She's not going to win this
fight. I know Natalie is tough, but even
she can't beat up destiny. And Sean
and I are destined to be together.

"So, what is it? You're the only one that
can be happy?" It felt good to break her
love high.

"It's not that I don't want you to be
happy but I want Sean to be happy too."

"And you don't think he would be happy with me?"

Natalie shakes her head. "No, because in the end, I don't think you would make him happy."

Now she's pissing me off. "How can you say that? I'm your best friend."

"That's how I can say it. Because I'm your best friend. Summer you need to figure out what you want in a relationship before you try to jump into another one. Sean figured that out. That's why he's happy with Alexis."

"Are we done?" I need to leave the room before I start crying like a baby.

"Yeah, we're done."

I walk for the door. "I'll see you tomorrow."

I walk out of the office and out of the back door of the store as quick as I can. My mind is racing thinking about what Natalie just told me. How dare she tell me I wouldn't make Sean happy? Every time we were together he was happy. I always gave him the goods the way he liked. Sean couldn't ask for a better lover. I was his first everything, including his first lingerie model. And I know I can cook better than Alexis. Sean never complained about my cooking. I kept him fed and satisfied.

And Natalie has the nerve to say I
wouldn't make Sean happy?
"What does she know?"
As I walk to towards the parking garage,
I think about what I want in a
relationship. I want what every girl
wants. Love, honesty, respect and
loyalty. Sean has all those qualities and
more. He looks good. He's successful
and he has his own home.   What more
can a girl ask for? Natalie is wrong. I
am not going to let Sean go without a
fight. I'm going to get Sean back,
tonight.

Chapter 11

Sean

After doing a little shopping and stopping by Cold Stone, Alexis and I make it back to the car and out the parking garage without saying anything to each other. I can tell she has a lot on her mind but she can't find the right words to say. I know what's on my mind, Summer. She looked good and smelled better. I wanted to stay there and be intoxicated by every bit of her. I wanted to get a love high so great I'd become a junkie for it. I wanted to take Summer somewhere and just sex her crazy like we used to do. But I can't do any of those things because I am committed to Alexis.

"So, Summer is cute."

Alexis catches me of guard. I was expecting her to trash talk Summer but

157

instead she gave her a compliment. I don't know if this is a trick to get me to say something incriminating about Summer.

"I mean, I can see why you were with her." Alexis says looking at me for a reaction.

"Yeah, she is cute, I guess."

Alexis laughs. "You guess. Come on now, Sean, you can't sleep with a girl for years and just guess she's cute."

I knew it. This was a trick. Alexis wants to know how I feel now that I've seen Summer. The truth is, I don't know. We really didn't get a chance to talk and all I could think about was how much I wanted to get inside of her. That's just my normal attraction to Summer. I've wanted to sleep with her since we were kids and when it finally happened, I wanted to do it over and over and over again. Nothing in the world felt better than being with Summer, that is, until I met Alexis. Now Summer may have been wilder in bed than Alexis, but Summer didn't always take the time to please me in every way. Sex with Summer was always all about her, but I didn't care as long as I was inside of her.

"You still want to be with her, don't you?" Alexis asks as I make a left on

San Pablo heading towards Forty-Third Street.

"Why do you keep asking me that?" I ask trying to get to the root of her insecurity, because now it's starting to annoy me.

"You're the one who said you weren't sure if you still had feelings for Summer. What? I'm supposed to just except that?"

I park on the street in front of my parents house and stay silent. I don't really know what to say but I have to get Alexis off of my back about Summer. I've tried and tried to make Alexis see that I love her and want to be with her but she keeps bringing up my feelings for Summer. It's almost like if I go and cheat then that would satisfy her. It's as if she's expecting me to cheat. So, why not do it? To her I already cheated when I told her I wasn't sure about my feelings for Summer. So if she already thinks I'm cheating in my heart, why not do the physical? It won't change anything.

She speaks, her voice calm. "Sean, I just want to know if I have anything to worry about. I've been hurt before and I need to know that you're not going to hurt me too."

I look at Alexis trying to find the right
words to say but I choose the wrong
ones. "For the past two years I've tried
to show you I'm not like the other men
in your life, but you don't believe me
when I tell you that I only want you. So
you know what? Until you can trust
me, maybe you should give that ring
back because I can't be with you if you
don't trust me."
There is a long, cold, tense silence in the
car. Alexis looks at her ring. I look at
her trying to figure out what's going on
in her mind. She probably wants to
curse me out, yell at me, hit me, throw
things, maybe even tear up my car. I
didn't want to say it. But, how many
times can I tell her I'm not cheating and
I'm not going to cheat before it becomes
annoying and too much? I asked her to
marry me because I knew right then
that she was the one woman I wanted to
spend the rest of my life with. But her
constant nagging has got me thinking
that Summer may be the better choice.
Alexis needs to make the decision of
whether she can trust me or not. If she
can't trust me, then we don't need to be
together.
A knock on the window breaks our
silence. It's Andrea standing on the
passenger side with a big smile on her

face. I roll the window down to see what
my little sister wants.
"Hey, I hope I'm not interrupting
anything, but I saw the car." She says
still smiling big.
"What's up, Drea?" I ask with a little
attitude.
"I just thought that since you guys are
back, Alexis could help with that one
move I can't seem to get."
I start to tell Andrea to come back
another time but Alexis cuts me off and
opens the car door and gets out.
"Come on, Andrea, lets go practice."
Alexis slams the car door and walks
away without looking back at me. I just
sit in the car thinking, but not about
Alexis, about Summer. I'm trying to be
a good, stand-up man and not go after
Summer, but she looked so damn good
today. It took everything in me not to
try and leave with her today. But the
way Alexis is acting right now, it would
be better if I go after Summer. She's the
one who wants me to confront my
feelings and her questions won't quiet
down unless I can honestly answer
them all.
I pull out my phone and call Summer.
She answers on the second ring.
"What's up, Sean?" The tone of her
voice has changed from sweet to

annoyed. She didn't even call me
honey.

"You busy right now?" I ask hoping she
would say no.

"I just finished with Nat. Why?" She
knows why and she's going to make me
work for it now.

"I need to talk with you. We didn't
finish our conversation earlier."

There's a long pause before she
answers. "There's nothing to talk about.
You're getting married. That's all I need
to know."

"What if there is more you need to
know?"

Summer sighs and sucks her teeth.

"Fine, Sean, meet me in about a half
hour. I live off of Broadway Terrace,
across from the Claremont golf course."

"Yeah, I know where that is. I'll be
there."

"I'll see you in a bit, Honey."

We hang-up. I look back at my parents'
place and see The Good Reverend
Winters coming my way. I begin to start
the car up and drive away but I decide
against it. Without asking, my father
opens the passenger door and sits.

"What's the problem, son?" He asks in a
concerned voice. It irritates me.

"Nothing, I'm fine." I tell him hoping he
would get out my car.

"Well, you have a good looking woman inside. Your mother made your favorite meal and you're sitting in the car looking like you've just got a call to deploy."

"You wouldn't understand."

After saying that, I want to take it back because he would probably understand. He was once caught up between two women and although I think he made the wrong choice, something good came out of it, my little sister. But do I really want to ask my father for advice? It would be like asking the enemy for help. I shouldn't feel that way but I do.

"You never talk to me, Sean. I know I've made some mistakes, but everyone has seemed to have forgiven me but you."

I wish I could forgive him but he nearly destroyed our family. He embarrassed us before the church and our family and friends. He made my mother raise a child that wasn't hers. He made me a target for jokes at school. And above all, he never apologized to me for all he put us through.

"You've never asked me for forgiveness." I tell him.

He looks at me for a second, but doesn't say anything. He's probably trying to think back to all the people he's apologized to over the years and trying to find when he apologized to me. He won't find a time because there isn't one. I guess he just figured I'd fall in line with my mother and just act like it never happened. But I know it happened. I'm reminded every time I think about Andrea and how she got here.

"Sean, I'm sorry, I never thought about it I guess." He says, trying to be sincere. "It's too late now, I shouldn't have had to tell you. Now if you would excuse me I'm going to take a drive." I tell him trying to get him out of my car.

He looks at me, then nods. He uses his cane to help him up and starts to close the car door. "I've been where you're at, Sean. Don't make my mistakes." He says as he closes the door and walks back to the house.

I roll down the window. "Tell mom to save me a plate. I'll be back in a while." He nods but doesn't turn around. I start up my car and head towards Broadway Terrace.

Chapter 12

Alexis

Andrea and I practice the praise dance downstairs in the small apartment. It's taken a minute but Andrea finally has the spin down. She seems to appreciate the time and patience I'm giving her and after about the fifth try, she finally got it. We both sit on the bed, sweaty and tired from dancing. The music still plays in the background as we try to relax. Andrea brought a bottle of water for us and I am enjoying a drink as it cools down my body.

"So what's it like dancing in music videos?" Andrea asks excitedly.

"It's hard work and you have to be selective in the projects you choose."

"What do you mean?"

"I never wanted to be just one of the booty shaking girls. I always chose my projects based on my role in the video. I was either a love interest or I was doing real choreographed dancing. Because choreographed dancing tells a story, booty shaking doesn't."

Andrea looks at me like she's the student and I'm the master. I feel like I have to tell her the truth so she doesn't end up like a bunch of girls I know. They get caught up in the life of hanging with stars and the glitz and glamour of it all. I've known too many good girls who got turned out and I was not going to be one of them. I notice a frown take over Andrea's face. "What's wrong?"

"Ever since I was a little girl, all I've ever wanted to do was be a dancer." She tells me. Her eyes stare into space. I imagine that she is thinking of the first time she discovered her love for dance. Then she looks down to her hands. "Dad just thinks it's a hobby. He's pushing me to be a business major."

I place my hand on her cheek and slowly guide her to look at me. I notice her eyes watering. Not enough to produce tears, but enough to give her a glassy look. I can tell she's in a battle. On one hand, she wants to make her father happy. But on the other, she wants to follow her heart and dance. She wants both hands to come together and shake in agreement. She wants to dance and she wants her father to be proud of that. I believe she should be able to do what she's passionate about. "What do you want to do?"

"I got accepted into San Francisco State University and they have a good dance program. But like I said, my dad wants me to focus on business." Andrea tells me with disappointment in her voice.

"Why not do both? I mean you can do a double major or major in one and minor in the other?"

Andrea shakes her head. "My dad doesn't think dance is reliable."

I smile. That's the same thing my big sister told me. "That's not true. I'm very successful. I bring home close to a thousand dollars a week teaching dance classes. Even more if I'm doing private lessons. To do a video makes me a little more depending on the project. And if I'm choreographing a video or stage performance, we're talking big money."

Andrea gets an excited look on her face but it disappears. "Dad won't go for it. Mom would though. She's been encouraging me to dance since I was five. But dad controls the money. He say's if he's paying for college, I have to major in what he wants me to major in. It's not fair!" She stands, folds her arms and pouts.

I can sense Andrea's frustration and I want to help. Maybe God has me here this weekend to help both Sean and Andrea get things right with their father. I've been where Andrea is. When I called and asked my sister for money to move to LA so I could become a dancer, she flat out told me no. She could have helped. She told me if I went to LA, the only dancing I would be doing is in a strip club. It's a good thing my Aunt believed in me and got me to LA and into an apartment with my cousin Simone.

I know Andrea feels she has to do what her father wants her to do. But I also know true happiness comes from doing what makes you happy, not what makes others happy. I knew I wanted to be a dancer from the time I was a little girl. It's all I could think about. It's where I found peace and sanity in my hectic and insane world. Some days when my mother was home she, would turn on the stereo and just start dancing with me in the living room of our two-bedroom apartment. My mother wanted to be a dancer, but being a very young single mother of three made it

impossible for her. Dancing was the
only time I ever saw her truly happy. It
made me want the same happiness.
"Why don't we go talk to your father
about this?" I ask.
Andrea shakes her head. "He won't
listen. Me and my mom tried to talk to
him about it. He says it's fine as a
hobby but I need to have a real job and
be like Sean and open my own
business."
"You can have your own business in
dance. You are your own business.
And you're as passionate about dance
as I am so I'm sure you'd be successful."
Andrea takes a long deep breath.
"Maybe I'll talk to him about it again. I
just can't see myself doing anything
other than dance."
I stand and walk to Andrea. "Don't say
maybe, do it. I'll come with you."
I hold my hand out for Andrea to take.
She looks at me for a while unsure of
what to do. I smile at her to let her
know it's OK. She reluctantly puts her
hand in mine. As I lead Andrea up the
stairs, my heart starts to beat. I don't
want to get on Mr. Winters' bad side, yet
at the same time I can't stand to see
Andrea give up her dream because he
can't see her passion. We get to the
second floor and walk right past Toni

who's standing at the stove frying chicken.

"Dinner's ready, girls." Toni says.

"We'll be there in a minute." I tell her. We walk to the office door which I found out earlier was Sean's old bedroom. Andrea tries to walk away but my firm grip on her hand forces her to stay. I can tell she's having second thoughts. To be honest, so am I. We both just stand at the door, neither one of us wanting to knock.

"What are you girls doing?" Toni asks from the kitchen.

I look back at her and smile. "About to become an adult."

I nudge Andrea. She looks at me, then rolls her eyes. She takes a deep breath, then lightly knocks on the door.

"Come in."

Andrea opens the door and she and I walk in. Mr. Winters looks at us and it looks as if he's scared at the ambush. He knows something is up and my guess is he thinks we're going to ask for something he doesn't want to give. I sit in one of the chairs in front of his desk while Andrea continues to stand. He takes his glasses off and sits back in his chair a little annoyed at the interruption. It looks as if he's working

on his sermon for Sunday's anniversary
service.

"How much?" Mr. Winters asks before
Andrea can say anything.

Andrea shakes her head. "I don't want
money, Daddy. I need to talk to you."

Mr. Winters changes his demeanor to be
more attentive. His baby seems like she
has something on her mind and he
wants to let her know he's listening.
"What's wrong?"

"I decided that I'm going to major in
dance and not business."

Mr. Winters looks at me with irritation.
"You put her up to this?"

I shrug my shoulders. "Yes and no...."

He cuts me off. "So is that what you
girls do? It's bad enough you dance
around in your underwear for the world
to see but you have to recruit young
naïve girls to do it as well? No daughter
of mine is going to become eye candy for
a bunch of horny, perverted men."

"Stop it, Daddy. That's mean."

I have to admit I'm a little offended and
ticked off. How dare he make an
assumption like that? I have never
danced in my underwear.

Photographed, yes. But I have never
danced around in my underwear for no
one except Sean. I feel my anger rising
but I keep a calm cool demeanor about

myself. "Have you ever seen my work?
Or, are you just going off what you've
heard?"

"Young lady, I don't need to see your
work. I've seen it all before you were
even born. Models are nothing more
than little sex pots that make men
fantasize about them."

"So, you've never fantasized about your
wife?" I ask deliberately trying to get
under his skin. Men hate when you
turn the tables on them.

"What kind of question is that? Are you
trying to get on my bad side?"

I stand. It's time to turn up the heat on
him. "All I'm saying is that beautiful
women are fantasized about no matter
what they do. Dancing and modeling
are all art. It's an expression of art and
Andrea is passionate about dancing."

Now he stands. It almost seems that if
he can't prove his point, he's going to try
and intimidate me by becoming bigger
than me. " I'm not going to talk about
this anymore. Andrea you are going to
major in business because that's
stable."

Andrea tries to stand up to her father.
"What if I go to business school and end
up opening my own dance studio?"

Mr. Winters is stuck speechless. He
looks at me again. "You've only been

here a day and already you've got my daughter thinking she wants to do something she doesn't want to do. Stop filling her head with thoughts that dancing is more than shaking your ass in front of people."

"Ronald!" Toni screams from the doorway.

We all look at Toni standing in the doorway with hands on hips.

Andrea turns back to her father. "Daddy, please listen. I want to dance as bad as Sean wants to take pictures."

"Dancing isn't the way to get it, Baby. Alexis sells an image of sex, that's all. That's not for you."

Andrea tears up and walks out of the office.

"Ronald, I'm not going to have you be disrespectful to Alexis. She is going to marry Sean. She's a part of this family now and you will treat her as such."

Mr. Winters sits back in his chair. "She can be a part of this family. Doesn't mean I have to like what she does for a living or allow her to convince my daughter to make poor decisions."

Instead of saying anything that might cause further arguing, I decide to walk out as well. As I walk to the kitchen I hear Toni scolding Mr. Winters. I start to think maybe Sean was right about his

father. I'm regretting my decision to
cancel our hotel reservations. If I
hadn't, I may be with Sean right now
making love instead of him being off
somewhere else right now.

I sit at the kitchen table and look at my
engagement ring. The princess cut two
and one half carat diamond ring is
everything I could ever want. But right
now I'm not very happy. I'm not stupid.
I know where Sean is. I'm well aware
the argument we had in the car did
nothing but push him away. It probably
made him think about all the good times
he had with Summer where there was
no arguing. I should have never told
Sean to talk to her to see where their
feelings were. I have a feeling that if
Sean talks to Summer it will be the end
of our relationship. I finally found a
good man and I pushed him into
another woman's arms and the thought
of Sean sleeping with Summer right now
keeps popping into my head.

Chapter 13

Sean

Summer texted me her address while I was on my way to her place. I stop by Jack'n'the Box on Telegraph Avenue and grab something to eat. I am starving and it also gives Summer time to get home and clean up a little. I'm pretty sure that's why she told me to meet her in a half-hour when it only takes about five minutes to get to her place from my parents. I can just picture it. She's running through the place picking up clothes and underwear. She's trying to put dishes in the dishwasher. She's wiping down her table and counter. I bet she's even putting all of her magazines in order.

As I sit and eat my spicy chicken sandwich and curly fries, I think back to how Summer always wanted everything perfect. Even her first time, even though it wasn't planned for us to lose our virginity to each other, it still came out perfect for both of us.

I remember it like my favorite song. It was prom night at the Marriot in downtown Oakland. I'd brought a date, a girl I'd gone out with a few times. Her name was Sonia White. She was cute and a virgin like me. I was sure the night was going to end with us in bed. I bought about six condoms just in case I broke the first few seeing as I had never put one on before.

Summer had come with her boyfriend of the last two years, Chris, aka Mr. Basketball, who was actually getting recruited by U. C L. A, Duke, North Carolina and Syracuse. Eric would joke with him saying he wasn't good enough for any of those schools. He and Summer had been together for such a long time that I thought for sure that they had started having sex. But that wasn't the case; at least the two of them weren't having sex together. Chris was having sex with a bunch of girls I knew about. Me, Eric and Natalie all tried to tell Summer but she was in love and couldn't hear us.

I remember Sonia was getting annoyed with me because I spent the whole night

taking pictures for the yearbook and she
wanted to dance. I couldn't help it
though. Pictures to me are memories
captured forever. It's nice to have good
memories, especially when you've had
some bad things happen in your life.
I was having a good time snapping
photos when I aimed my lens at
Summer and Chris in the corner of the
room. They were arguing and it looked
like it was getting heated. I started to go
over and break it, up but my mother
always told me to never get involved
with a couple's argument. You may
think you're coming to the woman's
rescue but she'll get pissed at you for
jumping in her and her man's business.
All of a sudden, I saw Summer mouth
the words "it's over", then walk out of
the room, nearly in tears. Chris looked
upset for a second until another girl
walked up to him and began to flirt.
Summer was quickly a distant memory
to him.
I look to the dance floor and see Sonia
had found another guy to dance with so
I didn't feel bad when I went after
Summer. I found her standing by the
elevators patting her eyes with a tissue.
I jog to her and get on the elevator just
before the doors close. She's quiet and

I'm not sure what to say so I do what I
do best and take a picture of her.
"Sean, that's not funny." She says
trying to fight back more tears.
"What's wrong, Summer?"
We reach a floor, I don't remember
which, but she gets off and I follow her.
We walk down a few rooms and Summer
stops. She pulls out her key card from
her purse and opens the door. She
looks at me for a few seconds then
walks in. A little unsure, I follow
Summer into the room. She throws her
purse on the nightstand and plops down
on the bed. I stand at the foot of the
bed and take another picture.
"Sean, I'm going to break that camera if
you take another picture." She says,
obviously annoyed.
"You want to be alone?" I ask. I don't
want to get on her bad side. I was just
concerned about her. I saw what
happened between her and Chris. It
looked as if she needed a friend. Natalie
and Eric were already gone by that time
so I guess I was it.
"If I wanted to be alone, I wouldn't have
let you follow me up here or come into
the room." She says, taking a deep
breath.
I know what's on her mind. Everybody
in the school had been talking about

Chris getting offered to play for U. C L. A and he was going to accept. If she thought his cheating was bad now, just wait until he's playing college ball.

"You guys were right." She says. "I knew he was cheating but I just thought it was because I wasn't giving him any. How did he expect for me to give him my virginity if he was always with another girl?"

That was news to me. I just assumed that Summer and Chris had started sleeping with each other just because they had been together almost two years. I guess I was wrong. So I'm not the only virgin in our group of friends. Eric had started as soon as he got his car at sixteen. Natalie had confided in me that she started having sex with her boyfriend earlier in the year. This made Summer even more beautiful to me because she didn't just give herself to anyone. She had respect for herself and I respected that.

"I thought for sure if I told him I would sleep with him tonight he would stop cheating. He told me I would always be his main girl and that any other girl would just be sex."

Summer looks at me with those big brown eyes filling with tears that she won't let fall. I want to hold her and comfort her. I want to make her smile again. I want to go back downstairs and beat Chris all the way up and down Broadway.

"I broke up with him. This time for good."

Summer and Chris always had an up and down relationship. They broke up at least once a month after he got caught cheating again. He'd buy her flowers and candy or dedicate a winning game to her and all would be forgiven. I guess she always thought he would change.

"I really thought tonight would be the night I lost my virginity." She says. She went on to tell me about how she saved up for months in order to afford the room. She even paid Natalie to make the dress she was wearing. Natalie usually didn't charge us. She also tells me how she bought condoms and lingerie for the evening. She was so excited about tonight, she let his flirting with other girls roll off of her back. But she said she caught him outside kissing another girl tonight and that was the last straw. She gave up trying to make him be someone he wasn't.

I set my camera down on the dresser in front of the bed. I take a seat next to Summer and give her a hug. I hold her firm as she squeezes tight. I rub her back for extra comfort. Her skin felt soft and smooth. I release the hug and wipe the tears from her eyes.

"Are you still a virgin, Sean?" She asks. The question caught me off guard. I wanted to tell her no and make myself seem like a bit of a player. I got a little nervous. The last time Summer asked me if I had ever done anything she kissed me. I started to think the same thing was going to happen and we were going to have sex. Those thoughts went to both heads and she noticed.

"You are aren't you?" She asks with a smile.

I start to stand but I decide against it. I figured it was best to answer while seated. "I had the same plan as you. But I doubt Sonia is going to be interested seeing as I haven't danced with her once tonight and I just left her to come see about you."

"Who would you rather sleep with, Sonia or me?" Summer asks.

I'm not sure if she's joking or being serious. Either way it wasn't a hard question to answer. Summer has been the girl next door since she moved next door. I've always had fantasies about sexing her more than any other woman I've come across. I remember she used

181

to let me suck on her tits a few years
back, but it never went any further than
that, though I wanted it to. Sonia, on
the other hand, was just a girl taking up
time as far I was concerned. I wasn't in
love with her; I barely liked her. She
was just a girl who said yes when I
asked her out on a date.
Summer puts her hand between my
legs. "I guess that's my answer," she
says as she leans in and kisses me.
"Summer, what are you doing? I
thought we agreed to just be friends," I
tell her not wanting to cause any issues
in our friendship, but also not wanting
her to stop.
Summer sits back and looks at me.
"You are my friend and that's why I
want to lose my virginity to you and no
one else."
I lean in this time and kiss her. I glide
my tongue into her mouth and play with
hers. She wraps her hand around neck
and pulls me to her. She leans back on
the bed and I climb on top of her and
rest in between her legs. I can't believe
this is happening and with Summer. I
was actually about to have sex with the
girl of my dreams. I tried to get my
mind off of it because I felt myself about
explode. Eric told me that you should

start thinking about other things so you don't give out too fast.

Summer pulled her dress down and her yellow skin revealed her soft breasts. They had grown since the last time I had seen them. I begin to suck the right, then the left, then back and forth for a few minutes as she goes crazy. I then look in her eyes and she bites her lip. She wanted me just as much as I wanted her.

I kiss her again as she takes off my tuxedo jacket. We both sit up on our knees as I get the jacket off. She quickly unbuttons my shirt as I unbuckle my pants. She kisses my chest then my neck, which almost brings me to climax again. I know something escaped before I could stop it. After a few seconds, I'm in nothing but my boxers as I pull her dress off slowly. I can tell she's still self-conscious about her body. She shouldn't have been, it was perfect. She was thick in all the right places and slim everywhere else.

She grabs her purse and pulls out a condom and hands it to me. I get nervous because I had never put a condom on before, so I started reading the instructions on the back of the package. Summer giggles at me.

"You don't remember sex class when
they showed us how to put the condom
on the banana?"
I actually think I was home sick that
day, but I didn't want to tell her that.
She sees me struggling and pulls my
boxers down, takes the condom out of
the package and slides it on me. She
smiles and looks in my eyes the whole
time. Once it's on, she lies back on the
bed. I pull down her sexy red lingerie
from Victoria's Secret. I climbed back
between her legs and pinch myself to
see if this is really happening. It is.
Summer helps me to find her secret
place. I slowly slide myself in and out
until both of us are comfortable with the
fit. Summer puts her hands on my
back as I move inside of her. We both
moan and groan for what seems like
forever. Finally, I couldn't hold it
anymore and I release inside of her and
collapse on top of her. She hugs me
and kisses my forehead.
"You're no longer a virgin, Honey," she
says as she kisses me again.
"Neither are you," I tell her as I slowly
pull myself out of her magical world and
lay next to her.
She lays her head on my chest.
"Are you okay?" I ask her, wondering if
it was good for her. Looking at the

clock, it only lasted about three minutes.

"I'm glad it was you," she says.

We kiss again, passionately, like lovers, which we now were.

"How do you feel?" She asks.

I look at her and smile. "I feel like I want to do it again."

She laughs at me. "I got a box full of condoms and the room for the night."

And that was our first time together. Although we never said we were boyfriend and girlfriend, we continued to have sex until we went off to college. Sonia didn't talk to me after that night. I guess I hurt her. And Chris made it to U. C. L. A. After college he got drafted to the Clippers and is now in three different custody disputes.

I pull into a guest parking space at Summer's condo, park and walk up a flight of stairs to get to her place. I pause for a moment before ringing the doorbell. I'm wondering if this is the right decision or am I walking into what could be the worst mistake of my life. On the one hand, I will finally know where Summer and I stand. On the other hand, I could be ruining my chances with a good woman already wearing my ring. If I choose not to talk

to Summer, then I'll always wonder
what if.

I take a deep breath and ring the
doorbell. I start to walk away when I
hear Summer call out, "Just a minute."
She sounds so sweet and sexy at the
same time. I know she's double-
checking her place to make sure nothing
is out of place. Everything always has
to be perfect for her. For as long as I
can remember, she has always been
such a perfectionist.

A few seconds pass and finally I hear
the door unlock and open. Summer
stands in the doorway in a pair of pink
sweats and a black wife beater. Her
hair is pulled back in a ponytail. All the
make-up she wore earlier has been
washed off and she only wears some
Mac lip-gloss. I don't know what she's
trying to get across with her outfit.
When I saw her this afternoon, she had
the tight grey dress and black boots and
her hair hung straight just above her
shoulders. She looked sexy then, but
now she looks beautiful.

I have to admit that I like when a
woman dresses up and looks sexy, but I
love when a woman is just laid back and
comfortable. Any woman can look
better with make-up but a beautiful
woman doesn't need it.

Summer smiles at me and I smile back. She reaches up and hugs me and gives me a kiss on the cheek. She then invites me into her condo. I look around as she closes the door. We stand in her living room, which has a nice love seat against one wall and a flat screen TV against the opposite wall. A glass coffee table sits in the middle of the room and two expensive looking grey chairs sit on each side of the love seat. Off to the right she has a nice size kitchen with orange pastel cabinets and stainless steel appliances. In the dinning room sits a glass table with four orange chairs.

"You want to sit?" She asks as she walks to her love seat.

I reluctantly walk over and sit next to her. The longer I sit next to her, the more I become intoxicated with her scent. The perfume she is wearing is driving me crazy. It makes me want to kiss her neck and taste her sweetness. We sit for a moment in awkward silence, not knowing what to say to each other.

"Why did you walk away from me earlier?" I ask her.

"Why didn't you tell me you were engaged?" She fires back.

I don't know how to answer because I honestly don't know the answer. When

Summer called me last night, I could have told her then, but I didn't. I could have told her while we were talking earlier, but I didn't. Maybe I really wanted to know what she wanted to talk to me about before dropping the bombshell. If she told me she wanted me back, then I would have no reason to tell her because I would have broken it off with Alexis. Or would I have?

"Look, you wanted to tell me something last night. What was it?" I ask trying to avoid answering her question.

"I wanted to talk about us," she says as she puts her hand on my leg.

I feel my temperature among other things rising. Her touch could bring me to climax but I hold strong, trying to be in control of this situation. If I lose control, I'll regret it, maybe.

"Summer, there hasn't been an us for over two years," I tell her.

"Are you really serious about getting married?"

"Why?" I'm curious, wondering if she is jealous.

"You've never been serious with a woman in your life, Honey. Except for me. I find it hard to believe you want to get married."

I look deep into Summer's eyes and say, "Maybe you should have been serious

with me and you just might be the one
who is getting married."
Summer drops her jaw and sits back.
"How can you say that? I was always
serious with you. You were my first
everything."
"But never your only."
I got her with that. Out of all the times
we were together over the years, she
always had another guy or two she
could go out with in case she got bored
with me.
"You were my only. The only one I truly
loved," she tells me as she gets close
again.
"Then why did you always brake it off
with me when another guy came
around?"
She puts her hand on the side of my
face. "Because I was stupid and I guess
I thought you would always be there. I
love you, Sean. Then and now."
Summer and I stare into each other's
eyes for a second. I start to look at her
soft pink lips. I start to lean in for a
kiss. She closes her eyes giving me
permission to go for it. I get so close I
can taste her breath. Then my phone
rings. The volume of my ring tone
startles both of us. Summer opens her
eyes and sits back. I lean back and

reach into the back pocket of my jeans and pull out my IPhone. It's Alexis. "You're not really going to answer that are you?" Summer asks with attitude. I can't ignore Alexis, that would just be wrong. I answer the call. "Hey, Lexis." "Where did you go?" She asks with a little irritation and concern mixed in with some hurt.

"I had to clear my head for a second, so I went for a drive."

"Look I'm sorry, Baby. I'm letting my insecurities get the best of me. I know you wouldn't do anything to hurt me. I love you."

That is weird, two women saying they love me within two minutes. I should be the happiest man in the world. Two beautiful, intelligent, independent women are really in love with me. I look at Summer who is irritated, rolling her eyes because she wants me right now. I have Alexis on the phone who wants me to come back to her right now. What's a brotha to do?

"I'll be back in a minute, Lexis. Okay. I love you too."

I hang-up the phone, making sure it's hung up and locked and put it back into my pocket. I take a deep breath and look at Summer.

"So, I guess you're going?" Summer
asks already knowing the answer.
I nod my head.
"You don't want to finish what we
started?"
I nod my head again. "I do, but I can't.
I can't leave this one for you just to have
to you break-up with me when another
man comes around that you like."
I kiss Summer on the cheek and stand
and head for the door. Summer stands
and stops me at the door.
"I'm sorry for hurting you, but the two of
us belong together. It's taken me a long
time to figure that out but I did. We're a
perfect fit and I want you as mine for
always. I've made you break-up with a
bunch of women for me but I promise
you that if you break-up with Alexis, she
would be last one."
"I'm sure you believe that."
I kiss Summer on the forehead and walk
out the door.

Chapter 14

Summer

"What the hell just happened?"
I was ready to prove to Sean that I loved
him by giving him the best sex he ever
had. How dare he walk out on me? I
walk to my freezer and pull out a bottle
of Ciroc Vodka. Regular wine is not
going to relax me tonight. I get some
cranberry juice out of the refrigerator
and a small glass out of the glass
cabinet just above the dishwasher. I
pour in the cranberry juice before the
Ciroc and mix it with my finger. I taste
my finger and am satisfied.
I walk to my bedroom only to be
disappointed. I got home quick. I didn't
need to straighten up because my house
is always neat. I was so excited that
Sean was coming over and wanted to

make sure it was special. I lit four
lavender scented candles in each corner
of the room. I had slow jams playing
low. The bed is made perfect, with the
comforter folded to the foot of the bed,
making it easier to get in then cover up.
I had some Africa's Best oil on the night
stand along with a bottle of Moscato and
two wine glasses. I was definitely going
to give Sean the night of his life. Damn
Alexis had to mess it all up by calling
my man.

"He doesn't know what he missed." I
say as I blow the candles out and turn
the music off.

Just looking at the room upsets me so I
go back to the living room, turn the TV
on and try to find something halfway
decent to watch on a Friday night.
There's a rerun of The Real House Wives
of Atlanta on so I decide to watch it. I
take a sip of my cranberry and vodka
and another and another and another. I
normally save my Ciroc for when Natalie
or some co-workers come over for girls
night. Usually, I just have a glass of
wine to relax in the evening. But
tonight I needed something to try and
make me forget that I was lonely. The
only problem is the vodka is making me
feel the need for some loving. And now

I'm mad because I was so close to
getting some tonight.

I can't figure out whether I'm angry or
hurt or both. I know I'm pissed. I put
all that work into making the bedroom
look special and Sean didn't even get to
see it. We were just about to kiss before
Alexis called and pulled him away. Out
of all the other times Alexis could have
come to town to visit, she chooses this
time. The time when I should have
Sean all to myself. That's my fault
though. Over the past two years, every
time Sean came to visit I made it a point
to miss him. I was so confused because
I wanted to see him each time he was in
town, but it just didn't seem right. The
last two times we talked he seemed cold
and distant. I knew he was serious with
Alexis so I passed the time trying to get
serious with my ex-fiancé, Jackson.
Thinking about Jackson only makes me
feel more lonely. Maybe I should call
him for a quickie since I had everything
ready for a sex fest and no one to share
it with. But that wouldn't be a good idea
because Jackson would think it was a
sign that we were getting back together.
And I have always vowed never to go
backwards, except for Sean. But that's
not going backwards because Sean has
always been there. Sean has been my

steady man since we were twelve and no one can come between that.

When a commercial hits, I go to the kitchen to refill my glass. I put the Ciroc back in the freezer hoping it will keep me from coming back for a third glass. I take a sip of my newly refreshed glass and walk back to my love seat just as my cell phone begins to ring.   A piece of me is hoping it's Sean telling me he's changed his mind and is coming back to help me release this sexual tension I have built up inside of me. When I pick up the phone and see the caller ID, I sigh, and answer my best friend's call.

"Hey, Nat." I was not in the mood to talk to anyone, especially Natalie who pissed me off earlier.

"Summer, I just wanted to apologize for earlier. I may have overstepped my boundaries telling what you should do with your heart and all."

"You're damn right you overstepped your boundaries!" I guess the vodka and cranberry gave me a boost of courage. Plus Natalie was on the phone and not in front of me so I don't have to worry about her slapping the hell out of me.

"Look, girl, I'm apologizing. Do you accept it or not?"

I pause for a minute trying to hold on to my anger but I can't. I've never been able to stay mad at Natalie for long. We've been best friends for fifteen years. Natalie saved me several times from getting beat up in high school when my mouth wrote a check that my ass couldn't cash. I love Natalie like a sister and I know she's only looking out for me, even if it seems she's more on Alexis' side right now.

"I forgive you, Nat."

"Good," Natalie says. "Now have you decided what you're going to do because I don't want any drama at my grand opening tomorrow?"

I tell Natalie everything. I tell her how I have done a lot of thinking and soul searching and realize that Sean is the one. I was too busy trying to explore that I pushed my one true love away. I tell her I'm scared that I may have lost Sean forever. I go into detail about my evening plans with Sean and how I had the bedroom set up for lovemaking and how right when we were about to kiss Alexis called and got Sean to leave before we had a chance to do anything. I tell her how Sean didn't hesitate to leave and how he told me that he wasn't sure if I truly wanted to be with him and only him.

"If he would have just let me put it on him, it would have worked and we would be in the middle of making love right now."

"It didn't work because you went about it wrong." Natalie finally has a chance to speak.

"What are you talking about?"

"You went into this expecting sex and not having a plan for the future. You need to tell Sean how you see your future with him."

I finish my second glass before speaking. "All a man needs to know is that the woman he's with is going to give him the ass when and how he wants it."

Natalie giggles. "See, that's why it was so easy for Sean to get up and leave yo ass sitting there lonely. He knows what the future holds for him and Alexis. All he could see with you is a quick lay."

I take offense to Natalie's statement. "I have never been a quick lay to anybody. I'm not a ho."

"Then tell me, Summer, why, when Sean has only been in town a few hours, did you have your bedroom set up for sex? What were you going to do afterwards?"

I can't answer Natalie's question because I really hadn't thought about the afterwards part. All I know is that I wanted to feel Sean inside of me again and make him forget about Alexis. But what would I have done after? Sean lives in LA and I live in Oakland. My pediatric practice is here and Sean's photography studio is in L. A. How would we make that work? Natalie is right. I don't have a plan for our future. I just know that my future wouldn't be right if Sean wasn't in it.

"That's exactly what I've been trying to get you see," Natalie says when I don't answer. "I can hear it in your voice that you're in love with Sean but you can't expect him to leave Alexis just because you throw sex in his face. You need to make him realize it wouldn't be the same old thing as before where you would drop him when another man comes around."

"I hear you, Nat. I hear you."

"Good. Now get some rest so you can be ready for tomorrow." Natalie says.

"Alright, girl. I'll talk to you later."

I hang up the phone trying to figure out my next move. I need to find a way to convince Sean that I will never leave him for another man again. How do I get him to see that he's the only man for me and has always been the only man for me? I have to come up with a better plan than just sex. I have to think about our future. The crazy thing is whenever I have thought about my future; Sean has always been in it, right beside me. Sean has always been the person I have felt most comfortable and safe with. That's why I ventured out so much. I was young and immature and being safe and secure wasn't so appealing. I needed a little bit of danger and drama to make me feel alive. But now I'm pushing thirty and being safe and secure is all I want. Sean is all I want.

Chapter 15

Sean

Driving back to my parents' place, I just can't stop thinking about what just transpired. I can't believe I just walked away from some free sex. It was right there for me to take it and I just walked away. Granted, my decision came from me not wanting to disappoint Alexis but still, I walked away from my first love, the girl of my dreams. Summer was ready and willing to give it to me and I walked away. What is wrong with me? I came up here to find out if Summer and I still had a connection and when I find out she still wants me, I walk away. I need to slap myself for not taking it when it was offered to me. Now I probably will never get the chance again. Although, knowing Summer, she always gets what she wants. So if she wants me bad enough, she'll try again before the weekend is over.

Trying to get my mind of off my poor decision, I put my Bluetooth in my ear and dial Melanie's number. I want to make sure my studio is still in tact and all went well with the shoot. I don't like letting people use my studio without me there, but I trust Melanie to keep things in order.

"Hey, Sean," Melanie answers, sounding a little winded.

"You okay, Melanie?"

"Yeah, just trying to clean up the studio, after the wild party we just had here."

"What!" I scream into the phone. "What party?"

I know they better not have thrown a party in my studio. I will fire both her and Miles. If they messed up my equipment, they are going to wish they were in another country. I don't play with my studio.

"Ease-up, Sean, I'm just joking," Melanie says with a giggle.

I don't find it funny, but I change my tone. "So everything went alright then?"

"What you thought? It wasn't?"

She tells me all about the photo shoot. She tells me that Miles is actually a good photographer and his wife was beautiful and should be a model. She goes on to explain that Miles has some real creative ways of shooting and that I should think about hiring him as photographer and get another assistant. "He's that good?" I ask.

"He may be better than you," she jokes.

"I'll look at his work when I get back. Not promising anything, but it may drum up more business having a third photographer. Lord knows I've been bringing in the business for us."

Melanie sucks her teeth before speaking. "Please! With all the artists Paul refers to the studio, I should be a partner in the business. Can you say fifty/fifty?"

"Whatever." I change the subject. "I ran into Summer up here."

Melanie takes a deep breath. She knows all about Summer. I talked about her all the time. Melanie never really put her opinion out there except once. She told me that Summer had me whipped. I told her I wasn't whipped, I was in love. But thinking back, maybe I was, maybe I still am.

"Don't tell me all your old feelings resurfaced and now you don't know what do?"

"You know me too well." I tell her.

"Does Alexis know about Summer?"

I tell her I've laid it all out for Alexis a long time ago. I told her that Alexis never seemed too worried about Summer until we got to Oakland. I even tell her about the encounter I just had with Summer and how I walked away. She quietly listens to me tell her the whole story as I park in front of my parents' house and turn off the engine. "I'm going to tell you like this, Sean, you're a good man and Alexis is a good woman and from what you told me, Summer is a good woman. What you need to do is to start thinking with your head, and not the one between your legs. The one between your legs will always get you into trouble but the one on your shoulders will give you clear direction."

She makes perfect sense. I mean the head between my legs only wants to go in one direction and that's the sweet spot. The one on my shoulders led me back to Alexis. I guess that's it. Alexis is the one I want to be with.

"I understand, Melanie, thanks."

"No, problem. See you Tuesday."

We hang up and I take the Bluetooth out of my ear. I know Alexis is the one for me and that she is the woman I am going to marry. I know this because I came back to her even when I could have had Summer tonight. I feel more confident in my decision now. I get out of the car and put on the alarm. I walk up the red stairs and ring the doorbell. Andrea opens the door a few seconds and a few locks later.

"Hey, Sean, your fiancé is cool. You better not mess this up."

I walk into the house and see Alexis and my mother sitting at the kitchen table. Alexis looks at me and smiles. She stands and walks over to the oven where a plate of fried chicken, greens and corn bread are being heated. Alexis takes an oven mitt from the side of the stove and pulls the plate out.

"We saved you a plate, Baby," Alexis says as she places the plate on top of the stove and closes the oven door.

"Where the heck have you been, Sean?" My mother says still sitting but glaring at me.

"I just went for a drive," I tell her

"You left Alexis here by herself. That's no way to treat the girl you're about marry, especially if this is the first time she's meeting your family."

I walk to Alexis and kiss her and hug her tight. "I know, I'm sorry."

"Me and Andrea had to keep her company. I'm sure she's tired of teaching dance moves and hearing my voice."

Alexis breaks the hug and walks to my mother and hugs her shoulders. "I could never get tired of hearing your voice. And I was glad to teach Andrea that dance step."

Andrea walks to the table and sits. "You made it look so easy."

Alexis sits as well. "It just takes practice. I've been praise dancing since I was a little girl."

"Thanks anyway, Sis."

Andrea is already calling Alexis Sis. I guess we're becoming a little family. I grab my plate of food and sit down in what is usually my father's chair, across from my mother and in the middle of Alexis and Andrea. I tear into the first piece of chicken and fall in love with my mother's cooking all over again. Even though I had a meal at Jack'n'the Box not too long ago, I made sure not to eat too much because I knew I wasn't going to get away with not eating my mother's home cooking.

As I eat, Alexis, my mother and Andrea continue to talk like they're old friends. My mother tells stories about me getting in trouble as a kid and how I would hide under my bed so I wouldn't get a whooping. It always failed though. I

always got it in the end. Andrea tells
stories about how I made her do
everything for me like she was my maid.
I made her clean my room and the
bathroom, even though we shared it.
I finish eating, stuffed to the top and
unable to move. I feel like unbuckling
my belt to release some of the pressure.
I'm ready to go downstairs and go to
sleep. Alexis yawns, signaling she's
tired too. It's not that late, only about
seven-thirty. I think the long drive wore
us out as well. Not to mention we didn't
get much sleep last night because we
were celebrating our engagement into
the wee hours of the morning.
"So, have you guys set a date yet?"
Andrea is so excited about me getting
married. She seems more excited than
Alexis.
Before I can answer, I hear the door to
my old room open up and my father
calls out. "Sean, can you come in here
for a minute?"
I wanted to yell out "Hell no," but I
decided against it. Alexis pats me on
my hand trying to get me to get up and
go talk with The Good Reverend
Winters. I take a napkin and wipe my
hands and mouth then reluctantly get
up and walk across the kitchen to my

father's office. I step in and close the
door behind me.

The Good Reverend Winters sits at his
desk going over notes. He looks a lot
older than what I remember. He has
more grey hair than black and he's
starting to move slower. At this moment
I almost feel a little sorry for him. I'm
trying to search my heart for forgiveness
for what he did but I can't find it. It's a
hard thing for a kid to handle when his
father disappoints him. My father
disappointed me, and he has tried for
years to make it up me but it hasn't
been enough.

"Sit down, Son." He gestures for me to
sit down in one of the chairs near his
desk.

I sit, trying to figure out what he called
me in the office for. I know I'm too old
to be in trouble for something like
getting a D on my report card. And I did
get a few of those.

"Sean, I know you don't think I meant it
when I said I'm sorry earlier, but I
wanted you to know that I am. I am
truly sorry for letting you down, Son."

"I just don't understand why you did it.
You're supposed to be a Christian leader
and you failed."

The Good Reverend Winters breaks
down the entire story to me. He says

he's not making any excuses. What he did was wrong and it was a moment of weakness. He tells how he's been faced with the temptation of many beautiful women in the church wanting to sleep with him. He told me how Andrea's mother was crying and needed comforting and the comforting led to them becoming intimate with each other. Afterwards, they both agreed it was a mistake and Tricia decided to find another church home.

Now my father could have not said anything and just let the transgression go. My mother would have never known, but he couldn't live with himself if he didn't tell her. He said he came home that night and told my mother the whole story. He said my mother was livid and was ready to head to divorce court the very next morning. My father slept downstairs that night and several nights after that. It took months before my mother decided to give him another chance and put the incident behind them.

Several months later, my father got a call from Tricia saying she was pregnant but didn't want anything from him. The only thing she wanted was to put his name on the birth certificate in case anything happened. It took another several months before my mother could forgive my father again, but she did. Then came news Tricia was killed during a car accident on the way home from work to get Andrea. Andrea was only four months old. My father got the call and since he was on the birth certificate, he was the legal guardian. He told me my mother made him go get Andrea but that she wasn't going to help him raise her. My father brought Andrea home and we all fell in love with her. My mother stayed true to her word for only a couple of weeks, but she couldn't help wanting to take care of Andrea too. After all, it wasn't Andrea's fault her parents made a big mistake. By the end of the story, The Good Reverend Winters was near tears. I too had watery eyes, but neither of us were going to cry. I have to admit after hearing the whole story, I wasn't as mad at my father. He did take responsibility for his actions. I stood up from my chair and shook his hand. The first time I had got this close to my father in years was right now. He stands and hugs me and apologizes again. I hug him back still trying to fight tears. I break the hug. "It's not going to happen over night but I'll work on forgiveness." I tell him.

"I'll take that, Son."
I look at the clock on his desk and see that over an hour has passed with his story. I walk out of the office and close the door behind me. The kitchen light is off and no one is to be found. I peek out the kitchen window and see Andrea's car is gone. She probably went out with some friends. It is Friday night. I walk to my parents room and hear a TV going so I figured my mother was in bed. I walk to the door that leads downstairs and open it. I close it behind me and lock it as I walk down the stairs.
Alexis sits on the bed watching the old TV that's off to the side of the dresser. She looks at me and smiles. I smile back seeing as she's only in her panties and bra and they are a matching purple set. It looks like she just got out of the shower. Her hair is wet and curly, and her body glows from baby oil and moisture. I begin to get excited looking at the woman I'm going to marry.
She breaks my train of thought.
"Andrea asked a good question tonight. I hadn't thought about setting a date for the wedding yet. What do you think?"
"I think you should ask me that question when you're not half naked." I sit on the bed next to Alexis and kiss her neck.

She gently pushes me away. "I'm being
serious Sean. I want to know what you
think."
I look at Alexis and say, "Septunuary."
She laughs and lightly slaps me on my
chest. I kiss her softly. I glide my
tongue in her mouth and play with hers.
"Promise me you'll think of a date," she
says with her hands around my neck in
between kisses.
"I promise."
We get back to kissing. I lean her back
on to the bed and climb on top of her in
between her legs.
"I thought you said the walls are thin
here. I don't want your mother and the
preacher to here us." Alexis has a not
so worried look on her face.
"We'll be fine, just internalize."
She giggles, then kisses me. I kiss her
from her head, to her neck, to her
breast, all the while making her hot.
She breathes deep as I get to her breast.
I pull the bra to the side and grab a tit
and put as much in mouth as would fit.
I suck hard on the nipple which makes
her go crazy. I rub her through her
panties and she gets juicy and I stand at
attention.
I pull her panties down, then kiss one
leg, then the other, then back and forth
until I reach heaven on earth. I begin to

kiss her lips. My tongue finds her pearl and I go at it like my favorite dessert, savoring every bite. Alexis takes some of the pillows and puts them over her face to muffle her moans. It doesn't take long for me to make her give me a brainstorm. Her body shakes and shivers as she tries to hold the pillow over her face and keep from screaming in excitement.

I smile and wipe the juices off of my chin. I smile at her as she finally takes the pillow from her face out of breath. She looks at me as if she wants me inside her more than ever. I'm pleased with how I've made her feel. Nothing pleases me more during sex than making my woman climax. She motions with her finger for me to finish the job. I pull down my jeans and underwear and climb on top of her. I enter her innermost walls slowly and gently because I know she's still sensitive. When I'm all the way in she puts her arms around my back and I begin to please her. Pleasing her pleases me. "Take your shirt off, I want my nails in your back." She says in between moans.

I get up on my knees, still inside, and with one arm pull off my button down shirt and under shirt and throw them to the side. I get back to business as Alexis digs her nails into my back. As I stroke, I kiss her neck. I can feel her about to get loud so I kiss her lips and make her bite my bottom lip to keep her quiet. I close my eyes and think about how good this is.

When I open my eyes I'm shocked to see Summer's face where Alexis' face should be. I start to pull out but decided against it. I make my strokes longer and harder not knowing if I'm trying to erase the image of Summer or if I'm trying harder to please the image of Summer. Whatever it is, I'm starting to make her get louder and louder and before I know it I'm exploding inside of her. My body weak, I fall on top of her as she kisses my neck.

"I love you, Baby." Alexis' voice comes out.

I lift myself up and see Alexis is the one lying with me. I'm relieved and disappointed at the same time. Relieved because I thought I was trippin' and may have been going crazy.

Disappointed because now I'm thinking maybe I should have slept with Summer one last time to get her out of my system. Unless I do it, I'm always going to think what if. Alexis is the woman I want to marry, but Summer is the one

that keeps me from giving myself fully to
her.

"I'm going to take a shower." I tell Alexis.
"I'm going to sleep. I hope your parents
didn't hear us."

I slowly pull out, get up and walk to the
bathroom and get in the shower. The
warm water fells good, relaxing. Too
many thoughts are running through my
head. Every time I try to push Summer
out of my head, she pops back in. I
can't seem to move past her. I want her
more than I knew. There is something
about Summer that makes me forget
everything and everyone else. For the
past two years she was the one who got
away. Now that I'm engaged, she seems
to be the one that wants back in. A
piece of me would love to have Summer
back with me but I can't see myself
without Alexis either. Both are good
women. Both really know me and love
me anyway. Both are smart, fine and
have a good sense of humor. Both
women are the only two women whom I
loved sleeping with above any other
women in my life. I can see myself
marrying and being happy with both of
them. Now I'm stuck and don't know
what to do.

I get out the shower, dry off and walk
back into the room, where Alexis has

passed out. I give myself a pat on the back for being able to put Alexis into a deep sleep so fast. I go to the dresser and pull out some boxers and a white under shirt. I pick up my pants from the side of the bed and pull out my cell phone and see that the light is blinking. I see that I have a text message from Summer.

It says: "I want you and you want me. Don't make the same mistake I made by walking away from us. We're meant to be. I love you, Honey."

I am not sure how to react or what to say. Summer has finally admitted she made a mistake in breaking up with me two years ago. Maybe she's finally come around and sees that she loves me as much as I loved her. We were good together when we were together. And even as friends we were great. I look over at Alexis who is letting out some loud snores now and think about where I see myself in the future. Do I want kids with Alexis? Can I grow old with Alexis? Will Alexis be there with me through the good and the bad? I don't know for certain. What I do know is Summer has already been there for me through the good and the bad. She helped me when I was struggling through school, gave me advice on love,

and taught me how to make love.
Summer has always been there and I
can't imagine her not being there. Even
though we've been apart for two years,
she's always been in my heart.
I look back at the text message, trying to
figure out how to respond. Do I tell her
to get over me or do I tell her to meet me
in an hour? I look back at Alexis who
looks so peaceful and beautiful. I don't
want to hurt her but I need to clear my
heart for either Alexis or Summer. I go
back to the text message and type in a
reply. "I want you. Let's see if we're
meant to be." I send the text, then place
my phone on the charger that Alexis has
put on the dresser for me.
I climb into bed and wrap my arms
around Alexis and feel the heat from her
body on mine. It feels good. She turns
to the side so that her ass is into my
stomach. I wrap my arm around to her
breast and grab it. It's so soft and feels
good in my hands. I hold Alexis tight as
I drift off to sleep. I wonder if this is the
last time I will hold Alexis. It's starting
to seem that by the end of the weekend
our engagement will be off and Summer
will the one lying in bed next to me.

Chapter 16

Sean

I wake up to my cell phone ringing. I quickly hop out of bed to answer the phone hoping it's Summer calling. I grab the phone from the dresser, disappointed to see it's Eric. My first thought is to ignore the call and get back into bed but I change my mind. "Hello."

"What up, family?" Eric says in an annoying happy tone.

I wanted to curse him out for waking me up early in the morning. I look at the clock on the nightstand next to the bed and see that it's eight 'o' clock. It's not too early, I guess but I was still tired. I look at Alexis who looks to still be asleep. She looks peaceful and beautiful. I've never seen a woman look more beautiful in the morning. It makes me want to get in the bed and get a

second round in with her this morning.
Thinking of that only makes me think of
seeing Summer last night while we were
having sex. The image of Summer made
me get more aggressive and made the
sex seem better.

"Sean, you there?" Eric asks.

"Yeah, I'm here, what's up?"

"Wanted to see if you wanted to grab
breakfast with me this morning?"

"Just me and you?" I ask.

"Yeah. Wanted to talk to you about
some stuff."

What is so important that he needs to
talk to me about it this morning? It
better not be any bull. I don't have time
for any drama. Knowing Eric he
probably wants to tell me about a new
girl he met and how he thinks she may
be better for him than Krystal. Eric
always has some type of drama going
on. That's one of the reasons he can't
bring himself to marry Krystal. He
always thinks there's something better
out there for him.

"When you want to go?" I ask him.

"Man, I'll pick you up in ten minutes.
I'm almost to your parents' place."

"Alright."

I hang up the phone and sit on the edge
of the bed. Alexis sits up in the bed and
stretches.

"Who was that?" She asks still yawning. "Eric wants me to go to breakfast with him. Said he needed to talk to me about something." I tell her.

She gets out of the bed and walks to the bathroom and closes the door behind her. I go to the dresser and grab a pair of jeans and my blue button down shirt. I begin to put on my clothes when I hear the toilet flush and the water in the sink start to run. Alexis is brushing her teeth. Her morning ritual despite the fact we're not home.

I think about how well Alexis and I know each other. Our routines, our little quirks, our pet peeves and how we're able to deal with them. I love the fact that she is so routine because it keeps me in a routine and on a schedule. With Summer it was different every morning because every morning was spontaneous. Some mornings she may wake up and make breakfast and some mornings we'd be each other's breakfast. Alexis hasn't changed her routine once since we've been together. As I finish getting dressed, Alexis walks out of the bathroom doing a yawn and stretch combo.

"How long do you think you'll be gone?" She asks.

I was expecting Alexis to ask if she could come. I was already trying to think of an excuse for her not to come, but I guess she already assumed she wasn't coming.

"I don't know, maybe an hour or two."

"Well, have fun with your friend. I'm going to go over the praise dance with your sister this morning."

"Okay" I say as I give her a kiss on the lips.

I walk to the bathroom to brush my teeth. Summer would have never let me kiss her first thing in the morning without brushing my teeth. She would tell me that my breath would get into her mouth and she didn't like the taste. Alexis doesn't seem to mind. After I brush my teeth and wash my face, I hear Eric's car pull in front of the house. Alexis is putting on a pair of jeans. I walk over to her and place my hand on her ass and kiss her neck. She turns to face me and kisses me on the lips.

"Have fun." She says as she kisses me again.

I leave out the private entrance of the transit apartment, close the door behind me and walk to Eric's Nissan Maxima. I get in the car and shake hands with Eric as he drives off.

"Sorry for the short notice, I just really needed to talk to you," he says as he turns down his music and makes a left on Linden St.

"What's up? It sounded hella important."

"Man, it's about Krystal."

"Don't tell me you cheated on her again. Eric has cheated on Krystal a few times that I know of because I had to cover for him. I don't know why he did it, but he did and got away with it almost every time except once. A couple of years ago, after I moved to LA, Eric had no one to cover for him and he made the mistake of letting the girl spend the night at his house, knowing full well Krystal had a key. She caught him red handed. It took months for Krystal to forgive him.

"Man, I haven't cheated on Krystal since the last time she caught me at the house and pulled out that knife. I thought she was going to kill me or chop off my boys, which would have killed me anyway."

It's good Eric learned his lesson. Krystal may talk a bit too much but she is still a good woman and didn't deserve to be treated the way Eric treated her. So my next question would be if he hasn't cheated on her, what is the

problem? I hope he's not thinking of
breaking up with her.

We make it to the IHOP restaurant in
Emeryville, which is just a few blocks
from my parents' place. Eric finds a
tight parking spot in the back of the
building. We get out of the car and
begin walking towards the restaurant.
Eric locks the car with the push of a
button. He then reaches into his black
sports coat and pulls out a ring box and
hands it to me.

I stop in my tracks as I look at the small
black box in my hand.   Eric stops and
looks at me while adjusting his black
slacks and straightening his yellow
dress shirt. I can't even speak. A part
of me wants to congratulate Eric on
taking the next step. The other part of
me wants to slap Eric and tell him that
he could never turn in his player card.
"Is this what I think it is?" I ask already
knowing the answer.

"Yeah, man, it is."

I shake my head as the two of us
continue to walk into the IHOP. We are
seated fast near a window towards the
back of the restaurant. I finally open up
the box and look at the ring. It's a nice
size, at least two carats, but probably
not totally flawless. I know if I couldn't
afford totally flawless, Eric probably

couldn't either. We make about the same amount per year.

"I bought it about three weeks ago; just been debating on giving it to Krystal," he tells me. He actually looks excited.

"Why you debating?" I ask him trying to get inside of his head.

If he bought this ring three weeks ago, he's obviously having second thoughts.

I had the same feeling going through my head when I bought the ring for Alexis.

I had the ring for only a few days, but if she hadn't found it, it may have been three weeks or more before I would have asked her to marry me.

"What if it's a mistake?" Eric says. His excitement is fading and the guy who is always joking is now serious.

The waitress comes and takes our order. I get the strawberry stuffed French Toast and Eric gets an order of pancakes. After the waitress takes our menus and walks away, I run down why Eric should ask Krystal to marry him.

The first and obvious reason to me is she's pregnant. The second reason is they have been together for a long time.

I explain to him that she has always had his back in everything and she is a ride-or-die type girl. She's faithful and above everything else, she loves him unconditionally.

"So you really think this is the right move?" Eric asks as our food arrives. "Yeah, Eric. You need to wife this girl before somebody else comes along." "Ain't no one else coming along. But I see what you saying."
We begin to eat and I ask Eric about Summer. He looks at me a little weird at first but then he understands where the conversation is going.
"You thinking about sleeping with Summer again, Sean?"
I look around to see if anyone heard him. No one seems to be paying any attention to our conversation so I nod.
"Summer is like a sister to me and I always liked you guys together, but man you're engaged now. Why would you mess it up?"
Eric makes a good point but he did also say he liked me and Summer together, which could be a sign that we are meant to be together.
"I don't think I can go and get married to Alexis if there is something still there for me and Summer."
"Sean, you know me. I'm always the one saying there is something better out there. So you do what you gotta do, Homie, and I have your back no matter what," Eric says as he finishes his meal.

As I get to the end of my French toast, I'm glad that at least Eric is on my side. He doesn't see anything wrong with me going after Summer as long as I'm happy. He's a true friend. I pull out my cell phone and text Summer: "Let's hook-up tonight". Less than a minute later I receive a reply from Summer: Let's. I don't really now what I'm doing, but I'm doing it.

Chapter 17

Alexis

I finish my morning quiet time with God
and now I'm ready to start my day. My
day always seems to go smoother when I
pray and read the word. Today I got
through chapters four and five of
Ephesians. I paid special attention to
chapter five where it talks about
marriage and what the duties of a
husband and wife are. A wife is to
submit to her husband. To me this
means being faithful and always having
his back and always helping him reach
his goals in life. It also talks about how
a husband is supposed to love his wife
like Christ loved the church and died for
it. To me that means the husband
should die to all other women and
should be willing to do whatever he has
to do to make his wife comfortable and

happy. I hope and pray Sean is that man for me.

The smell of coffee and bacon reach my nose which lets me know breakfast is almost ready. Andrea came down a few minutes ago and told me Toni wanted me to join them for breakfast and I agreed. My mother always told me never to turn down a free meal. Toni and Andrea have made me feel so welcome. I have fallen in love with these two women and am excited they are going to be my family. I just hope Sean's father comes around too and soon.

I get a little nervous about going upstairs. What if Sean's father is there? What will I say to him or what will he say to me? I sit on the freshly made bed and think about what happened last night between Sean's father and me. He really offended me and the old me was ready to curse him out, but I knew I had to keep my cool. I definitely didn't want to start any drama in the house and that's exactly why I didn't say anything to Sean when he came home yesterday. It was tough, but I was able to convince Toni and Andrea not to say anything as well.

After the whole incident last night, I had a great conversation with Toni and

Andrea. Toni kept apologizing on Ronald's behalf for his harsh words but I would rather hear the apology from him. There's no way a woman should have to apologize for her man's actions. He's grown and he should be man enough to admit when he's wrong. He need not only apologize to me, but also to his daughter whom he made cry. After Andrea had calmed down, Toni promised she would talk to Ronald about changing her major. Andrea felt a little relieved, but still didn't think anyone could persuade her father to change his mind because it was already set.

The conversation then turned to twenty questions about me and my life. They wanted to know everything about me, beyond the modeling and dancing, In an attempt to not over load them, I gave them the watered down version of my early life. I honestly felt if I told them too much they may think differently of me, or it may just bring the mood down too much. By the time Sean walked in the door last night, Toni and I had had a few wine coolers and were laughing along with Andrea like we had known each other for years.

After Sean finished his dinner and went into the office to talk with his father,

Andrea asked about Summer. She wanted to know if Summer and I had crossed paths yesterday. I told her we briefly saw each other at Natalie's store. Andrea spoke of her dislike for Summer. She said Summer used Sean, but for some reason Sean didn't care or couldn't see it. Andrea concluded with the fact she was happy Sean found someone who seems to really be in love with her big brother. I assured her I am crazy in love with Sean which made Toni smile and begin to tear up.

My ringing cell phone breaks my thoughts of last night. I get up from my sitting position on the bed. I grab the phone from the dresser and answer Simone's call.

"Simone, you're up early."

"That's because I've been up all night planning your wedding."

I laugh at my crazy cousin. Simone isn't one to play around when it comes to events. She has actually been planning her own wedding since she was twelve. Lord only knows what she's got in store for me. But she's moving a little too fast. It's barely been twenty-four hours since Sean and I got engaged.

"Cuz, we just got engaged less than two days ago. I haven't even set a wedding date yet."

"That's no problem. The wedding date is the third Saturday in June next year. It will be at our church and Pastor Tibbs will officiate. The color scheme will be purple and white and...."

I cut Simone off. "Hold on, Monie, don't I get a say in my own wedding? And what about Sean? He's not a fan of purple."

"All Sean has to do is stand at the alter and say 'I do'. As for you, all you have to do is find the right dress and I'll handle the rest."

"I appreciate the help, but lets discuss everything when I get home."

"You don't even want to know what kind of cake I picked out?" Simone asks, desperate to reveal her entire wedding plan.

"When I get home, Simone," I say with a little more sternness.

"Fine, I'll see you when you get back."

I end the call and place the phone in the back pocket of my tight jeans. I smile thinking about how good God is. I grew up with a sister who was so into herself that she never had time for me. If I tell her I'm getting married, she would make the whole thing about her. But Simone is looking out for me like a sister should. She knows purple is my favorite color and I've always dreamed of a wedding in a big church. Simone has been a blessing in my life.

I adjust my purple short sleeve top and walk up the stairs. I'm a little calmer and ready to handle what ever Sean's father has to say. I shouldn't be worried anyway; I just put on the whole armor of God. I'm ready for anything. The aroma of coffee and bacon gets even stronger on the second floor. Toni stands at the stove scrambling eggs, still in her robe and head wrap.

"Morning, Alexis. Breakfast is almost done."

I walk over to the coffee maker on the kitchen counter and grab one of the three cups in front of the freshly brewed coffee. I pour the coffee into the cup and add two teaspoons of sugar and powdered creamer, which is all set out. "Is Mr. Winters joining us for breakfast?" I ask.

"No, he went down to the church to prep everything for tomorrow's anniversary."

I feel a bit relieved. I don't want to feel any tension at the breakfast table. I especially don't want any drama to mess up the nice spread Toni has prepared. She has bacon, toast, pancakes, fresh fruit and is just finishing up with the eggs.

Andrea comes out of her room in a chipper mood. She has changed from the pajamas she wore when I saw her a few minutes ago into a short yellow dress with black tights and a pair of black flats. She gives me a hug and her mother a kiss on the cheek. She then grabs a coffee cup and repeats everything I did except she uses three teaspoons of sugar.

Andrea and I sit at the table in front of plates full of food. Toni brings over the pan of eggs and divides them among the three plates on the table. She tosses the pan into the sink and pours cold water over it to cool it down. She then grabs her cup and pours coffee into it adding nothing. She sits at the table and smiles at the two women who are not her biological daughters. She tells me she feels a new responsibility with me after finding out my mother passed away. The same motherly responsibility she felt for Andrea after her mother died. I start to tear up. Toni doesn't say anymore about it. Instead we turn our focus to breakfast.

"Alexis, dear, can you bless the food." I'm a little shocked at the request, but agree. We all bow our head as I thank God for bringing me into the Winters' family and for the love they have already shown. I bless the food and asked God to keep us all safe. The ladies say Amen and we dig in. As they eat, I look at Toni and Andrea, happy they accepted me into their family. Now I just want to stay in the family. I hope and pray Sean and I will make it through. I have a strange feeling Summer isn't going to make it easy. I know Summer wants Sean and that Sean still has feelings for Summer. I saw it when they looked at each other yesterday. I just hope Sean remembers he's engaged to me. Though when it comes to Summer, it may not matter.

Chapter 18

Summer

I lie in bed awake with a new attitude and a brand new mission. The text from Sean woke me up and it renewed my resolve to have him all to myself. I am going to prove to Sean I am the woman for him and I can be the perfect wife. I jump out of bed glad that I took two Excedrin's pills last night. The last thing I wanted to do was wake up with a hangover. I admit I went a little overboard with my drinking last night. Not my normal style, but I needed something to hide the pain of being alone.

I head to the bathroom and brush my teeth, wash my face and use the toilet before walking to my closet and picking out the perfect outfit to wear today. The weather report yesterday said it's supposed to be warm, so I pull out my blue jean skirt with a yellow short sleeve V-neck top and my yellow and white heels. Sean is going to go crazy over this outfit. It shows off my smooth, thick legs, which lead up to my nice round ass. The shirt shows the right amount of cleavage to make any mans mouth water. The heels make my ass stand up and demand attention.

I get a little moist thinking about Sean putting his tongue on my nipples and then on my lips. I had one sex dream after another last night about Sean. He was either on top beating my walls into submission or I was riding him hard and fast. I must have climaxed at least three times. All I can think about now is making my dream a reality.

I take off my clothes and head back to the bathroom and turn on my shower. I want to make sure I am totally clean and fresh for my man. As I step into the shower, my mind goes back to my conversation with Natalie. I realize now that I made some huge mistakes with men in the past and the biggest one was hurting Sean.

I knew from a young age that I was a beautiful girl, the kind a lot of men liked. I was light skinned with big juicy lips, big brown eyes, long hair and a big

booty. What can I say; I get it from my
mama. I saw the way grown men looked
at me when I would walk down the
street and I have to admit I liked the
attention. When I got to high school it
seemed like all the boys wanted to get
with me so I had my pick of the litter.
 I liked athletes and Chris was the best
basketball player in the district. I think
I went after Chris because unlike all the
other guys in school, Chris had all the
girls after him. It was more of a
challenge to make him mine. The only
problem was that he was never really all
mine. I caught him cheating several
times but I tried to ignore it. Prom night
was the last straw and I broke it off with
him. And Sean was there to pick up the
pieces. That is until I started college
and met Mark.
Like I said, I liked athletes and Mark
played football for Cal, drove a Camero
and had his own apartment. The only
thing Sean could offer me was his old
beat up car from high school and his
bedroom in his parents' place. Sean
had also started to become more
focused on photography and less on me.
To be honest, I couldn't see Sean
making any money in photography. He
was good, but athletes, to me, were a
sure thing. When I started seeing Mark

I stopped sleeping with Sean. A few weeks later I heard he was dating a girl who modeled for him. I was slightly jealous but I couldn't be mad.

Mark proved to be too cocky and emotionally abusive. Nothing I did was ever right and he told me time and time again I was not that good in bed. This fool had the nerve to bring another girl to his apartment to show me how to give him head. That night I left him and went back to Sean.

At the time Sean was talking to a girl named Melanie. He told me it was nothing serious and broke it off with her to come back to my bed. After about three months I was at a party Eric was hosting and met Duncan, a third string player for the Raiders. He had money, muscles and looks. I couldn't help but fall in love. Again I told Sean we had to stop sleeping together. Sean was little annoyed with me but I knew he wouldn't stay mad for long. Especially if I could get him and Eric free tickets to the Raiders' games.

It was bittersweet with Duncan. He took me on trips, bought me jewelry, paid for my hair and nails to get done every other week and even bought me a Honda Accord. The problem was Duncan was abusive, physically. At

first, it started with a pinch when I
didn't come home at the appointed time.
Then he started slapping me in the legs
and on the arms, but never the face. He
was extremely paranoid and constantly
blamed me for cheating when I wasn't.
I tried to keep the abuse a secret, but
Natalie saw a few bruises on my arm
one day and called in the calvary. I
tried hard to stop them, but Sean and
Eric showed up to Duncan's house and
promptly kicked his ass. I don't know
what they said to him, but Duncan
requested a trade and a few months
later found himself in Atlanta. I found
myself back in the protective arms of
Sean who made me feel important
again.
Life was good for about six months and
Sean even confessed that he loved me.
Even though Sean was good for me and
my self-esteem, he was still broke and
living with his parents.
As we approached the end of our fourth
year in college, Sean and I didn't see
each other much because of our
schedules. When we did see each other
we couldn't keep our hands off of one
another. We were becoming booty calls.
I didn't mind because it kept me from
stressing out over my senior projects. It
was hard to get together being that Sean

was at Cal State East Bay in Hayward
and I was across the bay in the dorms of
the University of San Francisco.
During my last semester I got into a
situation I shouldn't have. I took a class
on human sexuality with the very fine,
young professor Scott Hills. I made
several office visits to professor Hills
wanting help with assignments, but also
wanting to be in his presence. One
night while going over the study guide,
professor Hills made his move and
kissed me. I couldn't help but kiss him
back. We made love in his office that
night and every night thereafter for a
week. We started meeting in hotels at
his request. Our affair carried on for
the rest of senior year and I had finally
started to feel like I could love again.
Then I found out professor Hills was
married and had two kids.
When I confronted him about it he told
me he was separated and planning on
divorcing his wife and marrying me. I
believed him when he said he was going
to leave his wife but just wanted to
make sure his young children were
okay. I believed the lie until graduation
and I got my bachelors degree in
childhood development. At the
graduation I saw the love between
professor Hills and his wife, who was

pregnant with their third child. Heart broken, I ended it with professor Hills and went back to my Sean. That was short lived because a few months later Sean moved to Los Angeles to be a professional photographer.

Then I was shocked. I had no idea that while Sean was driving around in that beat up car for the past eight years and living at home that he was saving a lot of money for his business venture. From doing part-time work in the mall and taking pictures for family and friends' special events, he had actually saved thousands of dollars. He was lightweight balling and I never knew. This revelation turned me on and gave me motivation to visit Sean once in a while.

Sean had been in LA for a year before I met Nathan. Nathan worked at a bank and coached little league baseball on the weekends. I had fallen hard for Nathan and was ready to give my heart to him. I wanted to give my heart to Sean but he was hundreds of miles away. I couldn't see doing the long distance thing. It's one thing to visit every few weeks and have a weekend sex-a-thon, but it's another thing to be monogamous with someone who was not around. Nathan was tall, dark and handsome and I really wanted to see where things would go. Before I went for it, I made one more trip to LA to let Sean know I met someone else.

A piece of me wanted to see if Sean still loved me and that he may want to make what he and I had permanent. If Sean would have asked me to stay with him, I would have moved to LA and finished my schooling there. I guess I was looking for Sean to fight for me, but he never did. Every time I told him I met someone new he let me go without a fight. I guess I just figured he knew I'd always come back to him. I was never able to go back to him after my last trip to LA.

When I got to LA that Friday night Sean was busy with work. He gave me the key to his place and told me to relax and make myself at home. So I did just that. I found some ground turkey in the freezer and some elbow macaroni in the cabinet. I did have to make a quick run to the store for some tomato sauce and seasonings.   When I got back, I made a casserole, green beans, dinner rolls and a salad.

When Sean got home he enjoyed the meal I prepared and he enjoyed me for dessert. As I lay on my back with him deep sea diving, I realized how happy I was. I made dinner for Sean and was now being pleasured by the only man who truly knew my body inside and out. He ate me and I returned the favor. He always loved my oral pleasure. We went at it like two wild animals. There seemed to be extra passion between us. He pounded my walls into submission. I rode him until he couldn't hold on anymore and we climaxed together. Sean brought me to climax several times that night. He pleased me in every possible way. Our lovemaking was always perfect. I never had a complaint when it came to Sean Winters. He was blessed with looks, pipe and now money. I wanted to make him mine but I always questioned if he would fight for me.

The next morning, after we had slept in each other's arms, I got up and made breakfast. While Sean ate his French toast, eggs and sausage, I informed him of Nathan. I told him about how Nathan was a good guy and treated me nice. I don't know what it was but I really wanted to make Sean jealous. I wanted him to propose to me and tell me that he doesn't want me to be with anyone but him. He told me he loved me. I wanted him to prove it, but he did the opposite.

"So you just came here to put it on me and then go back to this new guy?" Sean asked in between bites.

"What, are you jealous? You want me to stay with you?" I asked while taking a sip of coffee.

"You do what you want to do, Summer. You always have," Sean said as he got up from the table and put his empty plate in the sink.

A little hurt and offended by Sean's comment, I chose not to say anything. Sean walked over and kissed me on the forehead. "I've got to get to work. If you're leaving, leave the key under the mat. Otherwise I'll see you later."

And with that Sean grabbed his camera bag and left without saying goodbye. At the time, I thought Sean's behavior was uncalled for. I did give him the opportunity to ask me to stay and he didn't. I was a little more than pissed that he didn't even seem to care. So I got up, washed the dishes, packed my bags and left his key under the mat and traveled back to Oakland to be with Nathan.

I actually thought if Sean wasn't the one for me then maybe Nathan was. But after only six months the relationship with Nathan fizzled because of our schedules. With him working everyday and coaching on the weekends and me in medical school and getting ready to apply for internships the next year, we never had time for each other. It was a mutual decision and neither one of us were mad. I was a little sad because Nathan was a good man. He just wasn't the one for me.

After the break-up with Nathan, I focused solely on medical school and getting an internship with Kaiser Permanente in San Francisco. During a short break in classes, I realized it had almost been a year since I had talked to Sean. He hadn't called me and I was too busy to call him. I heard updates from Eric and Natalie and knew he started dating a model but didn't know how serious it was. I got my internship with Kaiser and was doing great in school, but I hadn't had sex in close to six months after breaking up with Nathan. I decided that since I had a few days to relax I would go down to LA and get my freak on with Sean and then come back and get back to business.

When I called Sean to let him know I was coming down, he told me he was dating Alexis. That didn't bother me. I still wanted Sean to be inside of me. I told him that Alexis would never know and it would be just like old times. But

Sean told me the heartbreaking news that Alexis now had a key to his place and that they were practically living together. I didn't realize he and Alexis were so serious. And in my heart I just knew Sean would come back to me so I told him to call me when the relationship with Alexis had run its course. Obviously it never did and he never called.

With a little hurt from the rejection from Sean, I quickly got into a casual relationship with Jackson, a sports agent out of San Francisco. He and I met while shopping at Stonestown mall. We both had hectic schedules. Jackson traveled a lot and I was just about to enter my residency at Kaiser. But somehow we made it work for over a year. Jackson even proposed, but then the secret phone calls started and Jackson made the mistake of not cleaning his condo very well. I started finding jewelry that wasn't mine. I even found a pair of boy shorts; I wear hip huggers and thongs. Jackson finally came clean about his multiple affairs and promised after we got married it would all stop. I had played the fool before with professor Hills and I was not going to do it twice. I broke it off with

Jackson and have been single for the
past few months.

My daydream of boyfriends past ends
and I am now dressed and ready for the
day. I finish applying my make-up and
wonder if Natalie is right. Maybe I just
want to be with Sean because it has
been a few months since I got some. No.
I want to be with Sean because out of all
the guys I have ever dated, he is the
only one to make me feel safe, protected
and truly loved. I have been hurt too
many times and I'm ready to have a
man I know won't hurt me. Sean has
always been my man and now I need to
make him see that before he makes a
huge mistake and marries the wrong
woman.

I have no problem with Alexis as a
person, but there is no way Alexis can
love Sean the way that I can. There's no
way Alexis can sex Sean the way I can
either. I know him because I trained
him. We experimented together. I was
his first and I'm damn sure going to be
his last.

"It's time to take back what's mine." I
say to my reflection in the mirror.
Looking at myself in the mirror and
thinking about Sean putting a pounding
on my kitty has got me anxious.
Tonight is too long to wait. I want Sean

now. I walk out the bedroom and grab my cell phone from the charger in the dining room and dial in Sean's number. I already have a plan set. By this time tomorrow Alexis will be heading back to LA with tears in her eyes and Sean will be in my arms forever. The image of Sean in my bed makes me smile.
Finally Sean answers the phone on the fourth ring.
"Hey, Honey, it's me. I need to see you right now. Come to my place."

Chapter 19

Sean

I hang up the phone with Summer. She
sounds like she really wants to see me.
But I'm not in my car, I'm still with Eric.
"What was that about, Family?" Eric
asks.
"It's Summer. She said she needs to see
me right away."
Eric shakes his head as he turns onto
San Pablo. "What you want to do?"
I'm not sure. Eric was still nervous
about asking Krystal to marry him so he
wanted to kill some time by going to
Best Buy and possibly getting some new
electronics. Then he wanted to hit up
Office Max and get some supplies for his
office. "I'm kicking it with you man. I'm
trying to get you ready for your big
proposal tonight."

"Man I can handle it. I'll drop you over at Summer's real quick, do what I have to do and come back in an hour to get you."

I look at Eric for a second considering his offer. "You're an enabler, Bruh."

Eric nods and smiles. "Yes I am."

"Alright, let's swing by Summer's, but you stay in the car and wait for me."

"There you go, acting like the Sean I always wanted you to be. Go get you a little quickie and be back to your woman before she misses you."

I just shake my head and think about all the side women Eric had back in the day. He'd always have one main girl but at least three other women he could call to get a fix when his main wasn't acting right. The boy was a down right playa and I wouldn't be surprised if he still had a woman or two on the side now. It was always hard for me to juggle more than one woman at a time. Every time I tried I ended up getting caught after a few weeks. But Eric was slick. He never got caught, that is, until he met Krystal. Maybe that's why he's ready to marry her. Krystal is the only woman Eric couldn't fool or get to believe his lies. She sees right through him.

As Eric drives down 45th past Telegraph towards Broadway, I think about what

I'm doing. I can't shake the feeling that
this is a bad decision on my part. If
Alexis knew what I was doing she would
be pissed. But she is the one who told
me to confront my feelings for Summer.
How else am I suppose to know how I
really feel about Summer unless I talk
with her, kiss her, sleep with her? I
need to know if the fire is still burning
between us. I need to know if Summer
is truly the one for me.

As Eric parks in front of Summer's
condo, my nerves start to get to me. I
have a feeling that when I go up to
Summer's place I'm not going to be able
to help myself. We came close to kissing
last night and I don't know if a phone
call can stop me if our lips come that
close again. I look to Eric who is all
smiles, because he knows what's on my
mind. He's thinking, "go up there and
get you some then come back down and
give me all the details."

"Go on, Sean. What you waiting on?
You already got the invitation."

I look at Eric and nod my head. I get out
of his car and head for Summer's condo.
Walking to the front door, I imagine
Summer opening the door wearing
nothing but high heels, black or red,
doesn't matter. She'd done that a few
times when I would come over to her

apartment while we were in school. She would tell me she needed help with something to get me over to her place and when I'd ring the bell she would open the door butt naked except for a pair of black heels. One time we forgot to close the door and a neighbor saw the whole thing. It was little embarrassing, but the female neighbor did clap for us when we were through. And when I left she made sure to slip me her number, which I never used. Well, I did once after Summer moved out. But nothing happened, she'd gotten engaged.

I ring the doorbell and a few seconds later Summer opens the door. She is wearing a skirt with a yellow top that shows off her cleavage. She also has on some intoxicating perfume that makes me rise a bit. She looks me up and down stopping for a longer look at my bulge. She bites her bottom lip and stares at what she wants. She breaks her stare then steps away from the doorway to let me in and closes the door behind me.

I look at her and lick my lips. This woman drives me crazy. No matter how hard I try to deny it, all I want to do is be inside of her. I feel myself rising so I try to change my thinking, but it's too late. She sees and likes what she sees.

"Don't get all excited, Honey, I just said I
need to talk to you." Summer walks
past me to her love seat and sits.
I stand trying to will myself to go down.
After a few seconds of thinking about
business I feel myself shrinking back.
Summer motions for me to sit next to
her.
"You know what almost happened last
night when we sat next to each other?"
"Yeah, you left." She pats the love seat
again.
I walk to the love seat and sit. Her
perfume turns me on again. I look at
this sexy woman sitting next to me as
she smiles. She knows she finally has
me and this time I won't leave. I am
totally at her mercy and I don't mind. I
want to kiss her lips, then her neck,
then her tits, then her naval, then her
lips. I want to taste every part of her. I
want to make her scream my name as I
go deeper and deeper inside her walls.
And I know she wants it too.
"You left in such a hurry last night, we
didn't get a chance to really talk." She
begins.
"Wasn't sure if we were making a
mistake last night." I tell her.
I wasn't sure. I mean every part of me
wants to sex Summer down but is that
the only thing between us now, a

physical attraction? It's been two years since we've been together. Is that too much time? I've always loved Summer, from the moment she moved across the street from me. Summer was there for me when I found out about The Good Reverend Winters' affair. She calmed me down when all I wanted was to destroy something, hit something, curse out my father.

Summer would help me when I was struggling to pass classes in high school and college. She would always help me study even though she had a crazy class schedule herself. Most of all, Summer never ceased to surprise me in the bedroom. She'd pull out some new trick that would drive me crazy. Yes, sex with Summer was always awesome.

But now I'm thinking, what else besides the great sex was the attraction to Summer? Besides the fact that she is beautiful, what else did she really have to offer? The more I think about the good times we had, the more I think about the bad times. Summer actually hurt me every time she broke it off with me to be with someone else. I tried not to be insecure but I always felt like I wasn't good enough for her. I was just something to do until someone she really liked came along.

Trying to hide my hurt, I would just start dating girls I really didn't care about. I'd sleep with them but had no emotional connection to them. They were just something to do until Summer came back around. And as soon as Summer did come back to my bed, those other girls were gone, distant memories. It's sad when I think about it, but I don't remember some of their names because when Summer was with me, no one else mattered. But now someone else does matter. Alexis, my fiancé.

Summer puts her hand on my leg. "You wanted to know if I really loved you or if being with me would be like all the other times?"

Trying to keep myself from rising again, I simply nod trying to think of other things.

She continues. "I realize that it seemed that I was using you, but I wasn't. Or at least I wasn't trying to. I was young and dumb and wanted to explore. I needed more experiences. I didn't want to be settled at seventeen years old."

Summer goes on to explain that she knew I would always be around because I was a good and loyal man. She says she needed to date the other men in order to know for sure she had the right man in me. She goes on to tell me that she wished I fought harder for her and not let her go. A tear falls from her eye as she tells me that she is sorry for hurting me each time she broke it off with me for another man.

"I can't see being with any other man now, Sean. I love you and I'm sorry I didn't see it before." Tears fill her eyes. "I would die if you weren't in my life anymore. It's been killing me the past two years not being with you."

I wipe the tears from her eyes as I try to hold back my own. I have never heard Summer talk this passionately about anything other than becoming a pediatrician. I was not prepared for her to cry and to say that she can't live without me. Could it be true? The woman I have been after for half my life finally wants me and only me. I kiss her forehead then her cheek.

I whisper in her ear, "I've always loved you, Summer."

She turns her head and looks me directly in the eyes. "Then prove it and make love to me."

She kisses me. Her soft lips suck on mine. I kiss her back, passionately. She glides her soft tongue into my mouth and my tongue dances with hers in perfect harmony. She climbs on top

of me and straddles my lap. I put my
hands on her nice, round ass as she
grinds against my manhood. I squeeze
on her cheeks as our kissing becomes
more aggressive and our breaths more
labored.

Summer puts my head on her breasts
and I inhale her perfume, which she
sprayed right in the middle. "Yes, Sean.
Do it, Honey."

As I kiss her neck, my mind wanders to
the Good Reverend Winters and his
affair years ago. I think about how
much it hurt my mother and how I
never wanted to hurt a woman I loved
like that. Then I think about Alexis and
how much I do love her. If she knew
what I was doing right now, it would
break her heart. But I'm fighting a
losing battle because the wrong head
wants to do the thinking right now.

Summer jumps off of my lap and drops
to her knees. She begins to pull at my
belt. She unbuckles it and then
unbuttons my pants. I'm hard and
ready for whatever she wants to do right
now, but I can't get Alexis out of my
head. It's almost like she's haunting me
right now. Summer grabs my manhood
in her hand. She smiles as she begins
to pull it through my boxers and out
into the world.

I stop her. I grab her hand and pull it off of me. She looks confused and stands.

"What's wrong, Honey? You love when I give you a blow-your-mind blow job."

I stand and zip up my pants and buckle my belt. "I can't do it. Not right now at least."

"Are you still thinking about Alexis?" She asks standing herself.

"She is my fiancé."

Summer gets annoyed. "I just poured my heart out to you and professed my eternal love to you and you still want to go back to her?"

"Look, Summer, if the two of us are going to be together then I have to let Alexis know. It's only fair. And if we're going to be together, you need to think about what you want to do. Are you going to move to LA with me or what?"

"Why think about that now? I'm horny as hell and all I want is that big stick inside of me. We can make all the plans and break all the hearts after a round or two or three."

Summer's last statement makes me think that maybe she is just lonely and in need of sex. Perhaps she doesn't love me as much as she says or thinks she does. If she really wanted to be with me, she would have thought about everything and not just getting me in bed   She needs to do a little more thinking and we should talk a little more before we sleep together.

"I'm sorry, Summer, but if I'm going to break Alexis' heart, I need a reason other than you wanting to have sex."

Summer slaps me in the chest. "I just told you I love you! What else do you need?"

"We've said I love you to each other a ton of times and you still dated other men."

"Sean, you've dated other women. What's the difference?"

I gently put my hands on her shoulders. "The difference is that I never broke up with you to date those other women. I only dated them after you broke it off with me."

"And I apologized," she says with tears coming down her cheek.

I wipe the tears away. "I know. But you've burned me too many times."

Summer pushes my hands away, shakes her head and bites her lip. "The past is the past. I'm trying to start over with a future for me and you."

I know the past is the past, but the past keeps coming to my present thoughts like a still photograph. They say a picture is worth a thousand words but

memories are worth millions more. I
can't shake the memories of Summer
coming to me and coming with me, then
telling me that she met someone new
and couldn't sleep with me anymore.
After the last time she came to my
condo, made me dinner, then sexed me
like never before, I thought that she was
finally ready to commit to me. I was
finally ready to commit. My career was
taking off. I had my own home and was
getting ready to buy a new car. The only
thing I needed was a good woman by my
side and I hoped it was Summer.
Summer waited until the next morning
over breakfast to tell me she met
someone new. I was so pissed. I wanted
to curse her ass out or strangle her for
leading me to believe she was mine for
good. But I just left. A piece of me
hoped she would be in my condo when I
returned home that night, but I wasn't
surprised when I found she was gone.
That night I did a lot of thinking and
decided I was not going to let Summer
continue to come in and out of my life
anymore. I prayed that God would send
me a good woman who would not leave
me like Hosea's wife did him in the
Bible.
A few weeks later I met Alexis and have
been happy ever since. But now I'm

allowing Summer back into my heart
and I can't stop it. I have so much love
for her that I'm willing to let her hurt
me. Not this time. I can't let her
continue to use me for good sex then
leave without giving it a second thought
when the next rich man comes along.
Summer breaks my train of thought.
"What's is going to be, Sean Winters? A
future with your first and true love or a
future with the video vixen?"
"Let me talk to Alexis tonight and then I
can tell you where I'm at."
"So you're going to leave me here horny
again?" Summer says with her hands
on her hips.
The head on my shoulders says yes but
the head between my legs says no I'll
give it to you right now on your love
seat. I lick my lips and she smiles,
knowing what I'm thinking. She is so
damn sexy, but it's like she's the
forbidden fruit and I can't help but have
a bite. I look her up and down. She
walks to me and puts her hands around
my waist. She then takes one hand and
puts it on my manhood.
"He wants me, Sean. Don't deny him. I
know he's missed me."
I become weak as she squeezes me and
awakens me. "Hold on till tonight.
Everything should be settled," I tell her.

Summer pouts and gives me puppy dog
eyes. She then nods and kneels down
and kisses me though my jeans. "I'll see
you later tonight." She stands up
straight and kisses me soft on my lips,
invading my mouth with her tongue.
"I'll see you both tonight."
I walk to the door trying to fight the urge
to rip off Summer's clothes and beat her
walls up with straight jabs. As I get to
the door I turn to Summer. She smiles
then lifts her shirt and bra up and
flashes me. Her firm tits stand at
attention. Her brown nipples look at me
and almost put me in a trance. I open
the door and make a quick exit.
Trying to shake the thoughts running
through my head, wrap my head around
the fact that for the second straight time
I've walked away from free sex. This
time Summer was about to blow my
mind but I stopped her. Even though
Alexis didn't call this time, it was like
she was talking to me. I just kept
thinking about her and how the men
she's been with have done her wrong
and I don't want to be like every other
guy. In the same instance, Summer has
had some of the same luck with men
and I have always been her safe haven.
I don't want to hurt her either.

The problem is that no matter what, before this weekend is over, one of them is going to be hurt and I'm going to be the cause. Summer has always been the one I wanted from day one and I think she's finally ready to commit to me. Alexis is the woman who came into my life and made things make sense. She made me see that I don't have to live in fear of her leaving me for another man. She loves me.

I'm so deep in thought that I didn't realize that I walked past the guest parking area. I notice that Eric's car isn't there. This bastard left! I pull out my cell phone and see that I have a text message. It's from Eric saying that he went to Best Buy and Office Max and would be back in about an hour and for me to have fun.

"Damn, now how am I going to get to my parents' house?" It's a pretty long walk even though it's about five minutes in a car. I should call Eric and have him come back and get me but that may take a while.

Suddenly a car pulls up on the side of me. "You need a ride?" Summer asks. "Yeah, it seems like my ride left me." 'You know Eric. He's not one for waiting."

I open the passenger door and get into Summer's BMW. She smiles at me and drives off. I'm glad I have ride now and don't have to walk, but something doesn't feel right. It doesn't seem like a good idea to pull up in front of my parents' house in Summer's car.

Chapter 20

Alexis

After breakfast and a long talk with Toni and Andrea, I helped clean the kitchen then agreed to help Andrea wash her car. I feel at peace standing in the driveway on this warm summer day I feel at peace. I know I still need to find a way to be accepted by Sean's dad, but I believe it will happen in time. It had only been a day and Toni and Andrea made me feel like family. That's something I haven't had in a long time. "All done." Andrea says as she finishes drying the front window of her little Honda Civic.
"Looks good," I say, as we both admire the pretty red vehicle.
"So, do you have an idea of how you want the wedding day to be?" Andrea

asks as she pours the bucket of soapy water out into the street.

"I just want something simple. I don't have a lot of family. I know my big sister will come and I have a few relatives in LA." I tell her as I take the two dry towels and hang them on the railing of the stairs leading to the house. Andrea sets the bucket next to the stairs and wipes her hands on her pants. "I want a big wedding."

"You have some prospects?" I was curious. I have not heard Andrea talk about boys at all since we've been in town.

Andrea shakes her head. "I've been single for a while. I broke up with my last boyfriend about six months ago. He was trying to be too aggressive about having sex."

I look at Andrea in shock. "Are you still a virgin?"

Andrea puts her finger to her lips to quiet me. "Don't say it so loud. The last thing I need is for Mom to hear and start asking a bunch of questions. Then my dad will start giving me the birds and bees talk. Although his was called boys, girls and God."

I laugh. Still a little shocked. I didn't know anybody that stayed celibate through high school. I am sure Andrea

will have an experience or ten in college.
All I heard about college was it was an
all day sexcapade. I can't stop staring
at Andrea. I'm trying to figure out how
she was able to withstand all the
advances she surely gets. She's a pretty
girl and she's smart. I am certain boys
are after her all the time.

"Don't look at me like I'm an endangered
species," Andrea says noticing my stare.

"I'm just surprised."

"Don't be. My body, my decision. My
dad always said if a man isn't willing to
wait for it, he doesn't deserve to have it."

I nod in agreement. I think about Sean
and me and how he patiently waited for
me and how it had been the best
decision either one of us could make.
The wait made everything so much more
special. Waiting actually allowed us to
learn each other and fall in love with
each other and not in lust with each
other. I was totally in love with Sean
before we became intimate with each
other.

My sweet memories are broken by the
sound of R&B music coming down the
street. A silver BMW pulls in front of
the house and Sean is in the passenger
seat. To my surprise, Summer is in the
driver's seat. Now my mind begins to
race because Sean left with Eric this

morning. I saw him get into Eric's car, so how in the hell did he end up in Summer's?

I look at Andrea to see if she sees the same thing I see. Andrea has her mouth wide open and her eyes bugged out. I look back to the car just in time to see Summer give Sean a kiss on the cheek. Sean tries to avoid it but it's too late. Sean quickly gets out of the car and walks towards the driveway.

Summer rolls down the window and says, "Bye, Honey." She then gives me a wink and a devilish grin and pulls into her parents' driveway across the street. She gets out of the car and goes into the house using her own key.

Sean walks to me. "Hey, Lexis."

Sean leans in for a kiss, but I move away from him, trying my best not to yell and slap the taste out of his mouth. I feel my anger boiling and am ready to say the first four-letter word that comes to mind. How dare Sean show up to the house in Summer's car, especially when he was suppose to be having breakfast with Eric? He's got a lot of explaining to do and he better do it quickly before I find something to hit him with!

"You're an idiot." Andrea says.

Sean tries to play it off. "What?"

"If you don't know what, big brother, then you need to put yourself in Alexis' shoes. See how you would react if she showed up at your house in the car of an ex who kisses her and calls her honey."

"Quit trippin', Summer's a friend."

"Like I said, you're an idiot." Andrea grabs her keys off of the stairs, hops in her Honda, starts it up and drives off before Sean can say anything else.

Sean looks at me and I know he can sense I'm pissed. I am trying to tell myself I didn't see what I so obviously saw. But I can't erase the wink and the smile. It's the same wink and smile Summer gave me yesterday at Natalie's store. I have been wondering who the wink was for at the store, but now I know it was directed at me. Game recognizes game. Summer was working on a plan to get Sean, and from the looks of it, she might have succeeded. Sean's clothes look a little ruffled. There is a dark spot on his blue shirt, which could be make-up, and he smells like perfume that I don't wear. Obviously they were close, and recently. I fight the urge to pull down Sean's pants and do a sniff test.

"Lexis, nothing happened, okay." Sean tries to break the icy cold silence.

I stay and speak in a calm tone. "I thought you went to breakfast with Eric."
"I did."
Trying to keep from yelling and making a scene that would bring Sean's mom out and possibly some neighbors, I choose my words wisely. "Then tell me, fiancé, how is it that you were just dropped off by your ex-girlfriend?"
I can see Sean's mind racing trying to figure out the perfect lie to tell me. I don't understand why men try to lie knowing the truth will eventually come out. There is nothing that is done in the dark that doesn't come to the light. I've kept my calm demeanor for the past few minutes, but if Sean lays to me, I will definitely let him have it. There is nothing I dislike more in this world than a liar. If I can just meet one man that doesn't lie, then maybe I'll find the perfect man.
"You going to answer me or do you not have your lie straight yet?" I ask in a calm yet stern tone, after he doesn't respond to my inquiry.
Sean breaks down and tells me the whole story of how he went and saw Summer last night and they started to talk but ended up arguing. Then he tells me about how after breakfast

Summer called him and asked him to come over so they could talk again. He told me Eric was supposed to wait and the conversation would be short. He explains they came close to having sex, but he stopped and left. Eric was gone when he came out and while he was walking away from the condo, Summer offered him a ride and he accepted it. I listened, not saying a word, with my anger building and building. Sean cheated on me. He didn't have sex with Summer, but wanted to in his heart and that's just as bad. A piece of me can't blame him because I'm at fault too. I told Sean to confront his feelings with Summer. I pushed my man into the arms of another woman. I'm not sure what to think or feel right now. I'm angry with Sean for kissing another woman. I'm also mad at myself for telling him to go to Summer. Why couldn't I just be satisfied with the fact Sean put the ring on my finger? I just can't see marrying him if his heart is somewhere else.

"Baby, say something." Sean says trying to get a reaction out of me.

"You were going to sleep with her?" Sean nods. "I was, but I thought about hurting you and couldn't do it."

"Should have thought about me before you made the decision to go to her house last night. If at the first argument you're going to run to your ex, then what's the point of marrying me?" Sean puts his hands around my waist. "Because I love you and want to be with you. I made a mistake, but I'm admitting it and trying to move on." I move Sean's hands away and just stare at him. My eyes begin to fill with tears but I won't let them fall. I've done enough crying over men in my life and I'm not doing it anymore. I think about how good of a man Sean has been to me, faithful all the way, until today. Now I'm seeing him like all the other men in my past. They all cheat. Sean had just not had the right person to cheat with until now.

"Is she out of your system?" Sean nods. "I think so." I roll my eyes. "Not good enough." I take my ring off and hold it out for Sean. "You can give it back if and when you're sure."

Sean shakes his head. "You're not leaving me that easy. I waited a long time for you, you're mine." He says sternly. He kisses me on the forehead and lightens his tone. "We'll get through this."

Sean hugs me and I hug him back. I
look over Sean's shoulder at the house
across the street and see Summer
standing in the front window smiling.
Summer takes her thumb and wipes the
corners of her mouth, then winks at me.
She then closes the blinds of the front
window. I feel like running across the
street, breaking down the door and
throwing that tramp through the
window. Sean breaks the hug and takes
the ring from my hand and places it
back on my finger. I start to pull away
but decide against it. I love Sean and I
still want to marry him, but I'm afraid
I'm setting myself up for heartbreak.
"This is yours for forever." Sean kisses
me gently. "Lets go inside."
I melt at his voice and obey his request.
We walk into the apartment under the
main house. Sean closes the door and
leads me to the bed. He kisses me again
and picks me up in his arms. I don't
fight it even though I want to. Sean
places me gently on the bed. He
unbuttons my pants and pulls them
down. Next he pulls down my boy
shorts. He then proceeded to please me.
He kisses my lips then allows his tongue
to find my pearl. He lightly caresses it
causing me to begin the forgiving
process. As Sean kisses, licks and

sucks, I begin to feel more like Sean is telling the truth and that he really wants me and not Summer. I give in and allow Sean to bring me to climax. The anger and tension has been replaced by pure ecstasy.

Sean rises and wipes his chin, which is dripping with juices. He lays down on the bed next to me and holds me in his arms. I turn towards him and place my head on his rock hard chest and listen to his heartbeat, which always clams me down. Sean takes his hand and rubs my back, comforting and relaxing me. Hanging on to my anger would be pointless right now. At this moment I am the one lying next to Sean in nothing but a T-shirt and socks.

"I love you." I finally break our silence.

"I love you too," Sean responds and kisses my forehead.

Trying to get my mind off of the incident that just happened with Summer, I talk about something totally different. Trying to figure out what else to talk about is killing me because all I can think about is Sean kissing Summer and nearly sleeping with her. I take comfort in the fact he stopped and tried to leave. But, I can't shake the fact he put himself in that situation in the first place. He should have never let it get that far. Feeling my anger resurfacing, I decide to make light of my run in with Sean's dad.

"Your dad is quite a character."

"Oh, yeah, he says something last night?" Sean asks.

I tell Sean the whole story, starting from Andrea wanting to go to dance school and move to LA. I tell him about Andrea being scared of her dad and how I had to go with Andrea to talk to him about her dream. I try hard to turn it into a funny story by telling Sean how his dad got so angry and that he forbade Andrea to become a woman who sales sex like her.

"Wait a minute." Sean sits up in anger while I try to laugh it off. "Are you saying my dad called you a ho?"

Feeling I made a mistake telling Sean the story, I sit up and place a hand on his chest to calm him down.   The fire in Sean's eyes right now makes me think I may have to return the favor he just gave me to keep him calm. "No, he just doesn't understand what I do."

"So he feels he can just dictate what Andrea can do with her life and disrespect you without anybody saying anything?"

I can see it 's going to take more than my touch or a BJ to calm my man

274

down. "No, your mother gave him a tongue lashing last night."

Sean stands. "He's at the church, right?"

I stand still half naked and dripping a bit. "I think so, but I told you there's nothing left to say to him. I'm over it."

Sean heads for the door. "Oh, I'm not going to go talk to him, I'm going to do what I should have done years ago. I'm going to kick his ass."

Sean has an anger in his eyes that I've never seen before. It was the kind of rage I saw in my ex drug dealer boyfriend the day I saw him beat someone nearly to death for grabbing my ass in a club. It's the kind of rage you get when you want to kill someone. I wanted to calm him down. Here I am standing in front of him with easy access to my paradise and all he has to do is fall in. I want him to, but his anger is too far gone. Nothing is going to calm him. It's not the comment that made him so angry, but the comment was the last straw. Sean didn't say another word. He just walked out of the small apartment and headed down the street to his father's church. All I can do is watch. I can't run after him because I don't have on any pants. I say a quick prayer and start getting dressed.

Chapter 21

Sean

The heat of the afternoon and the walk
down to the church made me even
angrier. I can't believe The Good
Reverend Winters thinks he can just say
whatever he wants without any
consequences. He's always so quick to
judge people before he knows them and
his assumptions about them are usually
wrong. But now he's gone too far
because he's judging the woman I plan
to marry. He has no right to tell her
that her job is to sell sex. Her pictures
are always tasteful. Her video dancing
is art and choreographed most times by
her.

Just when I thought things might get
better between us, he goes and pulls
something like this. He talked to me
last night and never once mentioned his

words with Alexis. He got me to forgive him when he disrespected my woman an hour or so before. I almost cried with him last night, letting all my anger and disappointment dissipate after such a long time. Now he's going to feel my wrath. I'm going to kick his ass in his own damn church.

I walk up to the big, green church doors and walk in. The place looks totally different from the last time I visited about five years ago. There are holes in the walls and ceiling. The paint is faded and peeling. The red carpet is all torn up and has stains all over. My anger turns to sympathy as I walk throughout the medium sized church.

I walk to the kitchen and see the same old appliances and dishes I remember from my childhood. Nothing has been updated. Not the refrigerator, stove, nor the counter tops, everything is the same. There are ants crawling all over the place. It looks sad and definitely not a place where I would ever want to eat.

I walk to the bathroom that appears to have leaks at the sinks. The toilets look as if they haven't been cleaned in weeks. I turn the hot water knob on the sink but it doesn't turn on. The cold water does, however, come on with weak pressure. A cheap bar of hand soap sits on the sink with hair and dirt mixed in it. The smell of dried piss and sweat invades my nostrils as I look into the two bathroom stalls.

I walk of the bathroom into the lobby. I go through the double doors that lead into the sanctuary. The doors are uneven and don't close all the way. The carpet looks the same as in the lobby. The dark brown pews look old and chipped. Some of the pew benches are broken. The sanctuary could actually hold about four to five hundred. I walk to the pulpit where an old podium with an attached microphone sits. Behind the podium sit three chairs. Two small chairs and one large chair in the middle. Behind the chairs on a raised stage sits five rows of pews for the choir.

This is definitely not the picture of perfection I expected to see when I walked into the church today. I remember as a kid it being vibrant and full of life. The paint always looked good. The carpet never had a stain. How could The Good Reverend Winters let this happen to the church? It looks like some type of abandoned building with working lights. It doesn't make sense. One thing my father was when I was a kid, was anal about was how his church looked on the inside and out. I

was too mad to notice the outside, but
the inside slapped me in the face.
This is not the perfect image of God's
house. It has been five years since I've
stepped foot in a church. Alexis goes
every Sunday she's in town, faithfully.
Just knowing that the man who was
supposed to be our example could sin
made me think that every Preacher was
a hypocrite. My father turned me
against preachers and so called leaders
of the church, but not against God.
It seems like every few weeks I hear
about another scandal in the church.
Preachers are always getting in trouble
for sleeping with members, or stealing
money, or using drugs. I've even heard
churchgoers say some preachers just
teach the word wrong and are only in
the pulpit for show. And if my father,
who was my hero, could fail to do right,
how can I expect any other so called
men of God to do right?

My thing is that I will keep my
relationship with God between the two
of us and stay away from the church. I
feel its helped me because things have
been going great in my life. I have
everything I can possibly want right
now. But if I have gained everything
and my father has lost everything, I've

gained nothing. Despite my anger for what he did to my mother, my father was always a good provider. He took care of me. He paid my bills when I didn't have money. He paid for school the whole way so I didn't have to use financial aid. He even put a little money towards getting my studio started. I raised about twenty thousand from working part-time and doing pictures for people on the side while I was in school. It was my father, however, who co-signed the loan that helped me get all equipment and start up cash I needed to run the studio.

Looking at the church, I feel it's my turn to take care of my old man and his dream, because it looks as if it has all fallen apart. I walk to the back of the church towards the stairs that lead to the administration offices. Three small offices sit on the second floor. One being the finance office, which my mother runs. The second being the assistant minister's office, though I don't think my father has an assistant minister at the moment. The third office is, of course, The Good Reverend Winters' office. There is also a small conference room set up for meetings and small Bible study classes.

As I walk up the stairs, I hear my father's voice, but can't make out who he's talking to. As I get closer to his office, I realize he's not just talking, he's praying. His voice sounds shaky and almost as if he's praying and crying at the same time. I don't want to be rude and eavesdrop on his conversation with God, but I can't help but hear what he has to say. I walk slowly and quietly towards his office door and see him sitting at his desk, his chair turned to face the wall.

"Father, I thank you for all that you've done. I thank you for bringing my son this weekend. I hope that we can begin to rebuild our relationship. I pray that Alexis is the woman you have selected for him and that she would be a good wife and friend for him. And then, Father, I ask that you allow this anniversary set for tomorrow to go off without a hitch. I know that things haven't looked so good for the last few years, but I know it's going to get better. I just pray sooner than later. You've kept the doors open thus far, but with our dwindling membership and falling behind on the rent, I don't know how much longer we can last. Your house is falling apart and if it's due to my past transgressions I pray that you don't punish your people for my mistakes. This church needs you right now and I know that you are an on time God so I will leave it all in your hands. These and all blessings I ask in Your Son Jesus' name, Amen."

He finishes his prayer and turns around to see me standing in the doorway. He looks at me a little shocked. I guess I startled him. After seeing the church and hearing his prayer, I don't know if I still want to beat him or hug him. We stare at each a long time. He may be wondering if I'm there to jump on him or not. Perhaps he can see in my eyes that Alexis told me what happened last night.

"What's going on, Sean? What brings you down here this afternoon?" He breaks the silence.

I walk into the office trying to bring my anger back to the forefront of my mind. "Actually, I wanted to talk to you about your talk with Alexis last night."

His eyes get big. He knows he should have said something last night. He probably figured since the women didn't say anything, why should he worry about it? What was said and done was said and done. "I thought that might come up."

"What's wrong with you? I try to give us a chance to have a relationship and you disrespect my woman. Then you try to demand that Andrea do what you want her to do and not what makes her happy."

"I got this from your mother last night." He says motioning for me to sit.

I sit in the chair in front of his desk.

"Now you'll get it from me. Tell me what is wrong with you so that I can know whether I can continue to be in your life."

The last statement hit him pretty good. We haven't been on good terms for a while but I still talked with him and saw him every once in a while. Now he was facing not seeing me ever again. And if that happens and I have kids, he'll never see his grandchildren.

He begins by telling me he fears of losing Andrea to LA like he lost me. Andrea was the child he was able to be truly close with because there has been a barrier between the two of us for years. He also tells me that he knows Andrea can dance, but doesn't think she'll be able to make a living doing it. He goes on to say that he's scared of what the future holds for him and his church. He says that Andrea has been a bright spot in the church because of her praise dancing. If she leaves, that will be the final straw in his church going under.

"What happened to the church? You never said anything to me about it falling apart."

"It was none of your concern, Sean. You had your life to live and I didn't want to get in the way."

"But I have a little money now. I could have helped raise more to keep the maintenance up. It looks horrible down there."

"How do you think I would feel going to my son and asking for money?"

"Like a man admitting he needs help. This is crazy. You'd let your church fall apart before allowing your pride to ask for help?"

He sits back in his chair. "Would you have helped me? You barely talk to me anymore and when you do it's always cold."

I stand, knowing that I've held visual animosity towards my father for years. He hurt my mother and I have not been able to forgive him and I don't know why. My mother has forgiven him and even helped take on the responsibility of his mistake. Maybe that's a question I need to ask her and then maybe I could learn to forgive him.

"Sean." Like God had heard my
thoughts, I turn around and see my
mother and Alexis standing in the
doorway.
"Mom, what are you doing down here
with Alexis?"
Both women walk into the room. "Alexis
told me you stormed out of the house
and was heading down here with fire in
your eyes. I guess I'm the extinguisher."
Little did she know, but the images of
the church quenched my burning desire
to hurt The Good Reverend Winters. I
look at Alexis as she nervously stands
by the door, hoping fireworks weren't
about to start. I hold my hand out and
she walks to me and takes it.
"I have a question for you, Mom."
"Oh Lord, let me sit down." She sits on
the couch against the wall of the office
where my father takes a nap sometimes.
"What made you forgive dad and stay
with him all these years? Why stay if he
cheated."
The Good Reverend Winters looks at her
as if wanting to know the answer as
much as me. My mother looks at me as
if she's wondered why it took me so long
to ask, or maybe it was a look of why
did you ask me at all. She looks at my
father and smiles, which shocks me. I
would expect her to get angry when

thinking of my father's affair eighteen
years ago.

"Sean, it wasn't easy. It took a lot of
prayer and patience, but above all else,
it was God and the fact is your father
has never lied. He's always been honest
even when he's done wrong."

She goes on to explain how she was
ready to divorce my father immediately
after finding out about the affair, but
when Tricia disappeared, she felt as if
that part of their life was behind them
and they could move on without worries.
Then, when she found out about
Andrea, and that Tricia died, she didn't
want to help raise my father's baby.

She said for weeks my father got up
whenever Andrea cried in the middle of
the night. He did everything for the
baby without any help from her. My
father was preparing sermons, making
meetings, teaching Bible study and
teaching at the Bible college. He would
then pick Andrea up from day care or
my aunt's house and bathe, feed and
put Andrea down to sleep.

My mother goes on to tell us that one
night when she knew my father was
worn out, Andrea started crying and The
Good Reverend Winters slowly started to
get up, almost zombie like. My mother
put her hand on his arm and told him to

sleep and she would handle her. When she went into the room to get Andrea, she held her in her arms for the first time and fell in love. She said she fed her and changed her diaper and just stared at the child who was beginning to look like her mother. She said she saw past Andrea's looks and saw her as an innocent child in need of a mother's love.

From then on, my mother began helping more and more until Andrea became more like their child than the proof of my fathers infidelity. She finally decided to adopt Andrea since she had taken on the role of mother anyway. She said it was never Andrea's fault and she never wanted to be resentful towards her. That's why she considers Andrea as much her daughter as I am her son.

"Sean, above everything, I stayed with your father because I knew that no matter what happened, he would be honest and tell me the whole truth. That's the most important thing in relationships, open and honest communication."

The Good Reverend Winters chimes in. "That's true, Sean. Open communication brings total honesty and honesty brings trust. I made a mistake and paid for it. I had another mouth to feed and send through school. I also lost church members and respect in the community. As you can see, the church house has suffered as well."

"Communication, honesty and trust kept you guys together?" Alexis asks still holding my hand.

My mother nods. "Yes, and our faith helped us weather that storm and all others."

I look to my father, finally seeing him as a good responsible man and not just a preacher who had an affair. He's a man who made a mistake and he's not the only one. Even though he's a preacher, he still has a sin nature like all of us. He's basically a sheep himself. It's just he's been called by God to lead the sheep. I understand him more because I'm having the same issues right now, having two different women at once.

I look at my watch. "I have to get Alexis over to Natalie's store, but Dad, we need to talk about how we're going to fix this church up and get it back to what it used to be."

He smiles and nods at me in agreement. I walk to my mom and kiss her on the cheek and thank her. She hugs me tight and gives me a kiss on the cheek as well. I look at Alexis and smile. I take her by the hand and lead her out of the church and down the street to my parents' place. She runs into the house to grab some make-up and a change of clothes.

I look across the street and see Summer's car is gone. I think about what my mother said about staying with my father and having open communication. I think about what happened between Summer and me this morning and how much I hurt Alexis because of it. Even though I didn't sleep with Summer, the sting of my desire was enough to hurt Alexis. It made me not want to put myself in that situation again. So I have decided that I'm done with Summer and that I only need Alexis. But man, it would have been good to sleep with Summer one more time.

Chapter 22

Summer

I stand in Natalie's office wearing a beautiful green and brown evening gown. I remember Natalie using me as a model a year ago when she designed this dress. This was the only dress I wanted to wear tonight, even though there are two different outfits Natalie wants me to wear for the grand opening. I think back to all the times I've modeled for Natalie. Ever since we were teenagers Natalie has used me as her live mannequin.

I was actually excited about modeling for Natalie tonight, that is, until I found out Natalie had become buddy-buddy with Alexis. Ever since I arrived at the store an hour ago all Natalie has been talking about is how great it was going to be to have a professional model her clothes. She also talked Sean into taking some pictures, which he may be able to sell to a magazine or something. Natalie had a little power couple making all her dreams come true.

I stand and stare into the full-length mirror on Natalie's wall next to her desk. I love the way I look in this dress. I love the soft fabric on my skin. The dress hugs all my curves. The green and brown heels make my ass sit up nice. I really feel like a princess. Now all I need is my prince, Prince Sean, by my side and all will be right with my kingdom.

Suddenly, Natalie bursts into the office looking stressed but smiling. "There you are girl. Why aren't you in the dressing room changing with the other girls?"

I shoot Natalie an angry look. "I don't want to change in the room with The Model."

Natalie closes the door. "Quit tripping. She ain't even here yet." Natalie walks in front of me and my reflection in the mirror. "Now I told you and you promised not to start no drama tonight. We open in one hour and I want it to go off with out any problems or I'm going to kill you."

The last statement wasn't true, but I know Natalie would be highly upset if her opening night was ruined. And if I were the reason it was ruined, Natalie would probably kick my ass all the way to Texas. She need not worry though. I have no intention in causing a scene tonight. However, if all goes right, I will be leaving with Sean and Alexis will be on her way back to LA alone.

I have it all worked out. It is the perfect plan and I plan on executing it with precision. I am on a mission tonight and no one is going to stand in my way; no one is going to stop me from getting what I want. Sean has always been my man. I just never saw it before. But now that I know what I want, and that is Sean all to myself. I have nothing personally against Alexis as a person, but when it comes to Sean, Alexis is the enemy.

"Summer go get ready. I need you guys in place." Natalie says as she tries to gently push me to the door.

"Alright, fine. I'll go put on my make-up."

I leave Natalie's office and walk down the hallway to the private dressing room which is actually the employee break room. At the moment it's empty. The other two girls must have walked out

into the store or went to the rest room.
The dressing/break room is small. No
privacy from the other's in the room. It
has a small table sitting in front of a
mirror where I sit and begin applying
my make-up. Just as I finish putting on
my earth tone lip stick, Alexis walks in,
stops and stares at me for a second
before putting her things down on a
round table in the middle of the room.
"Hi, Alexis," I say with fake enthusiasm.
"Summer," Alexis, says trying to be
cordial but not friendly.
Alexis begins pulling out her make-up
and avoids eye contact with me. I apply
green eye shadow, trying to match my
beautiful gown. For a moment I catch
myself staring at Alexis. She's so
beautiful it's sickening. Flawless skin,
small but full lips, perfect thin nose and
gorgeous light brown eyes. The only
things I have that are better are my ass
and tits. Her thin ass is no match for
my juicy booty and C-cup breasts.
Before I can take my eyes off my
nemesis, she catches me staring at her.
She doesn't say anything, but her
silence is speaking loud and clear.
She's about to let what little street she
has come out. She doesn't take her eyes
off of me. Finally, I let out a little giggle
and turn my attention back to my

make-up. I decide that now it's time to put the next phase of "Operation Get Sean Back" into action.

"Does Sean still do that lick then suck, lick then suck motion I taught him?" I ask with out looking at her.

"Summer, don't start. You can stop with the fakeness around me. I get enough of that in Los Angeles. You don't have to like me, but you should know I'm going to be around for a long time."

I turn to face Alexis. "Excuse the hell out of me! I was just trying to make sure a sista was getting it right."

"I'm wearing the ring. I'm getting it right and he must be too to wife me." Alexis shoots back.

I just smile. I got under Alexis' skin, which is exactly what I wanted to do. Now it was time to go in for the kill. "So when Sean kissed you, how did I taste?"

Alexis drops her make-up and starts to walk towards me, but stops when Natalie and the other two young models walk into the dressing room.

"Alright ladies, we're about to open the store so lets go over your roles for tonight." Natalie says in an excited yet nervous voice.

Alexis walks to the other side of the round table and sits with her back to me. I can tell she's pissed and that makes me happy. The other two girls sit in the two chairs next to Alexis. Natalie doesn't sit. She seems too nervous to sit or even stand still.

"Alright ladies, we have less than an hour before the doors open." Natalie begins. "So, you know that you all have three outfit changes, first the evening gowns, then the 'N' jeans and T-shirts and finally the lingerie."

Natalie goes on to explain the purpose of each outfit and why she's going in the order she's going. Basically, she wants to show her elegant side first because that's what she's known for. The Jeans and T-shirts are to show that she's still down with the everyday female who wants to dress down but still look cute. The lingerie is for the men as much as it's for the women, and it's Natalie's newest venture. She just started designing teddy's, mini dresses and garters this past year. A few discreet clients have asked her to design something sexy for their husbands or boyfriends. It turns out lingerie may be her biggest seller.

"Any questions ladies?" Natalie asks at the end of her speech.

No one has any questions. The other two girls and I were already in their gowns but Alexis had just gotten there and wasn't ready. Natalie shows Alexis her dress. I watch as Alexis puts on a purple dress that has one of the shoulders out. I have to admit, Alexis looks good in the dress. It hugs her curves perfectly; her arms and legs are well toned and even have a beautiful glow. When she puts on the purple heels Natalie picked out, they show off her sexy calf's and make her butt stand at attention. Heels and form fitting clothes tend to help women with little booties like Alexis.

I begin to feel myself become jealous, but I have to stay on mission. I know I have Alexis flustered and now I've put the idea in her head that Sean and I had sex, even if Sean told her we didn't. It will make the next move perfect, but the next move will have to wait a while. First I need to get through Natalie's grand opening with no problems. Alexis puts on her make up with a small compact she has in her make-up bag. Natalie tells us all to get into place. Alexis and the two girls follow Natalie out the room to get into place. I wait until they walk out then I make my way over to Alexis's purse that's sitting on the table. I open it and pull out Alexis' cell phone. I take the phone to my

purse on the table where I was doing my
make-up. I place the phone in my purse
and look in the mirror and smile.
Natalie walks back in. "Summer, will
you come on!"
I blow myself a kiss in the mirror and
turn and walk out the room with
Natalie. I look good and feel good. My
plan is working out perfectly. If it keeps
going the way it's supposed to, Sean will
be snatching that ring off of Alexis'
finger and putting it on mine. Phase
one, two and three have already been
executed. Not it's time for the fourth
and final phase. Phase four ends with
Sean making love to me tonight, in the
morning and for the rest of our lives.

Chapter 23

Sean

I snapped pictures of the guests, the models, Natalie and her husband Charles all evening. I haven't worked this hard since the last wedding I did a month ago and I'm not even getting paid for this. Since Natalie is my friend and has done a lot for me over the years, the least I can do is make her night as memorable as possible. I snap shots that will bring back memories of all the laughs, joy and excitement. I capture several special moments in time. They say we don't have a time machine, but photos take us back in time whenever we look at them.

And to think, I almost forgot my camera at my parents' place. I was in such deep thought I didn't think to go inside to get my camera bag. Alexis and I were in the car halfway to the store when she asked me if I put my camera in the car. I had to turn around and go back to my parents' place to get it. Then I got into a conversation with Summer's mom who was sitting on her porch drinking what she said was lemonade. The lemonade seemed to make her a little too happy. By the time I got to the store, Alexis was late and it was all my fault. I apologized to Natalie, but she didn't seem to care. She was just glad Alexis agreed to model for her.

As I snap shots of Natalie's models, I can't help but take more of Alexis than any others. Summer had her fair share of photo time as well, but I think subconsciously I was trying to avoid Summer. I wanted to focus on Alexis, my fiancé, the woman I plan to marry. I have to admit, I've been nervous all night because I thought Summer would say something or Alexis may get mad and the two might start fighting. But the night has been peaceful and civil. The grand opening seems to be a huge success for Natalie and I'm very proud of my friend. Several customers have bought gowns and some have bought jeans. Natalie has sent the girls back to change into their last outfits for the evening. I take a break and walk over to

the bar where Eric is serving up wine
and champagne for Natalie's customers
and guests.

"What up, Family? You come for some
champagne or wine?"

"I came to ask why you left me stranded
earlier?" I had not yet had the chance
to talk with him about that whole
situation and what happened when I
went into Summer's condo.

Eric smiles at me, knowing he was
wrong, but thought he was doing what I
wanted him to do. "I figured you were
going to be a while."

"Come on, Eric, you know I'm about to
get married man, that's not cool. You
set me up for failure."

"Dude, you set yourself up for failure by
going over there. Plus you told me to go
anyway."

I look at Eric for a second trying to
figure out where he remembered me
telling him to leave. I told him to stay,
so what happened wouldn't happen. I
know I didn't tell him to leave, but he
seems to think I did.

"Eric, I didn't tell you to leave."

Eric pulls out his cell phone and goes to
a text message and hands me the
phone. I see that the text is from
Summer and it says: Eric, Sean says to

come back in a while, he'll text you
when he's ready to leave.
I hand the phone back to Eric. "I never
told her to send you a text."
Krystal walks over to us. I give her a
quick belly rub. I know that must drive
pregnant women crazy, but I just can't
help it. I look at her finger and see that
the ring Eric had earlier is now placed
prominently on her Krystal's ring finger.
I grab her hand and look at the ring. I
give her another hug and congratulate
her. I turn to Eric and shake his hand.
"I didn't know it went down already."
I'm guessing he went home and asked
her after he left me.
"Man, Family, when you didn't call me
back earlier I had extra time on my
hands and just decided to go for it."
"I told him no at first." Krystal says
with a light giggle. "I thought he had
done something wrong."
"Yeah and I told her I was finally doing
something right." Eric says as he grabs
a glass and takes a sip of the
champagne he's supposed to be serving.
"Well, I'm happy for you guys."
"We're happy for you." Krystal says.
"And I'm sorry if I said too much earlier.
You know how I get to talking." She
walks to Eric who puts his free arm

around her and kisses her on the forehead.

I tell Krystal I forgive her and that it wasn't a big deal. Then I see Alexis, Summer and the other models come from the back office area in some sexy lingerie. I couldn't help but stare. I turn my camera on and speed walk towards the models. I begin to snap shots of the women as they pose for the customers, guests and me. Other folks have taken out their phones and are taking photos too. Natalie has security quickly make them put their phones away.

Alexis smiles for my camera. I can tell she's getting turned on. She has been since I started snapping pictures of her when the store first opened. Not to mention the fact that Eric has supplied her with two glasses of champagne during her wardrobe changes. She wears an orange teddy and matching panties with orange and white heels. As I watch Alexis in her lingerie, I think about taking her to one of the back rooms and giving her the best of me. I try to stay in work mode but it's hard, very hard when Alexis is standing there looking edible.

I try to divert my attention and take pictures of the other models. Summer

looks good in an all white mini dress
and white heels. She blows a kiss. I'm
not sure if it's for the camera or me.
More than likely it was for me, but I'm
moving on. I have a good woman that I
don't want to hurt. I continue to snap
for a few more minutes then turn my
attention to the customers who are all in
the lingerie section trying to find the
perfect set for their men.

After about ten minutes, Natalie allows
the girls to go to the back and change
into their regular clothes. Natalie
planned to keep the store opened for
another two or three hours but she
didn't want the models to freeze in their
lingerie.

I walk to Natalie who stands towards the
front of the store taking pictures with
customers and guests. Charles stands
off to the side. I walk to him and shake
his hand.

"She finally did it." I tell him.

"Yeah, she's finally got it opened."

"So does that mean you get your house
back? I know she's moved all of those
mannequins and sewing machines out."

"Man, no. She still designs at home, but
she promised to spend more time
working here and not at home. Do you
know how hard it is to watch a football

game while she's sewing something?"
He says shaking his head.
I know Charles didn't mind too much.
He was drunk in love with Natalie.
From the first time he asked her to
dance at a club seven years ago, he was
in love. He gave her some corny line,
but Natalie thought he was handsome
and she agreed to dance with him. After
the club they talked for a while outside
then exchanged numbers and continued
to talk over the phone. Finally, Natalie
agreed to go out with him and within
four months she was talking marriage,
although the wedding didn't happen for
another two years. They've been
married the last four or so years and
seem to have it all together.
"So, what's marriage like?" I mean you
two seem to be happy."
Charles looks at me in the eye. "It's like
completion. You know how you can
have everything going your way, but still
feel like you haven't got the one thing
you need to make it complete. When I
married Natalie, I felt complete."
I give him dap. "That was deep."
"That was truth," he says as Natalie
walks over to him and kisses him and
then hugs me.

"Sean, thank you so much for taking pictures tonight. I really appreciate it," she says.

"No problem."

I feel my cell phone vibrate. I pull it out and see I have a text from Alexis: Meet me in the break room." I smile. I turned her on out here when I was taking pictures of her. Now it's time for me to turn her out in the break room. I tell Natalie and Charles I'm going to go to the rest room. I give my camera to Eric to watch for a few minutes. I walk to the back, shaking hands with a few customers of whom I took pictures during the evening.

I walk to the break room, but the door is closed and locked so I knock twice. The door suddenly opens and I walk in. I don't see anyone at first, but then the door closes behind me. I turn around to see Summer standing at the door wearing nothing but the white heels, her body oiled up and shining

"Summer, what the hell?" I scream as she starts to walk towards me.

"We didn't get to finish what we started earlier at my place."

I back up trying to distance myself from Summer. I don't see the chair behind me and I trip and fall to the ground. Before I can get up, Summer is on top of

me, kissing me. I try to get her off, but I
can't get a grip on her oily body.
"Stop fighting it, Sean. You know you
still want me. Once you taste this
sweetness again, you'll remember."
Suddenly, and before I can do anything
about it, Summer straddles my face. I
inhale her as she slowly grinds her lips
on my nose and lips. "Summer stop."
She doesn't. She has my face on her
lips and is trying to get me to taste her.
A piece of me wants to give in and kiss
her lips, but I know I can't. I made a
promise to Alexis and to myself.
The next thing I know the door opens
and Summer jumps up quickly looking
for something to cover herself with. I
wipe my face and sit up and look at my
future walk away. Alexis just saw me
face first in Summer. How am I going to
explain that? I get up as Summer puts
on the skirt and shirt she had on earlier
today.
"What the hell were you thinking,
Summer? Why would you do that?"
"I was thinking, that if we did it, you
would remember how good it was. How
we used to be, before Alexis."
I get angry but try and keep my voice
down. "Summer, it used to be because
it's in the past. I wanted only you for
years, but you just never wanted me.

Now that I have someone who wants me
as much as I want them, you decide you
want me? It's too late. I tried to see if
there was something between us, but all
there was is sexual attraction. Alexis is
the one I want to be with, not you. You
waited too long to show me you loved
me. Alexis showed me first."
I walk out of the room leaving Summer
standing there alone and heartbroken. I
hope she doesn't cry, but right now
she's not my concern. I need to find
Alexis and tell her what happened. I
walk out to the store and see no sign of
her. I walk over to Eric ask him if he
has seen Alexis.   All he does is hand
me her engagement ring.
"Where did she go, Eric?"
"She just asked Krystal to take her to
the airport." He tells me. "What
happened? You two have a fight?"
"Finish taking photos with the camera.
I gotta go get her."
I run out the store hearing Eric say
something smart but not really caring. I
need to find Alexis. I need to make it
right.

Chapter 24

Alexis

Krystal pulls her Nissan Murano in front of Sean's parents' house and puts it in park. I sit in the passenger seat wiping tears from my eyes, even though they keep falling. I can't believe I just caught Sean cheating on me. After all of his talk about how he only wanted to be with me, he ends up being like all the other men in my life. I forgave him for his slip earlier because I felt I had part to play in the situation. He promised me that she was out of his system as we drove to Natalie's store. I see that was all a lie. Summer flat out told me Sean went down on her earlier. I tried to ignore it, but after what I just saw, I can see she's telling the truth.

I try to regain my composure and not make such a scene in front of Krystal. "Thank you for the ride, Krystal." Krystal has a look of concern on her face. From what Sean has told me, she's been in my shoes before. "No problem, girl."
I reach for the door to open it, but Krystal puts her hand on my arm. I turn to face her trying to fight back tears. Krystal opens her arms wide and I go in for a hug. It was a difficult hug because of Krystal's expecting tummy, but it made me feel a little better.
"Don't worry, Alexis, everything is going to be alright." Krystal says with all sincerity
I break the hug and smile at Krystal. I believe the two of us could have been good friends. I get out of the car and walk to the house. Krystal drives off when I get to the downstairs apartment door. At first I wanted Krystal to drive me to the airport, but I didn't want to be rude and make her miss the rest of the grand opening. So I just asked her for a ride to Sean's parents' place and I would call a taxi when I was done packing. Toni had given Sean and me each a key to the downstairs apartment so we would have access when she or her husband weren't home, which they

weren't at the moment. I walk in and turn on a light. I walk to the closet and grab my suitcase and begin packing with tears still streaming down my face. The image of Summer on top of Sean naked and riding his face turned my stomach. I feel my heart beating faster as I imagine what they had done earlier in the day when Sean said they only kissed. Was he lying? Had there been more? Have they been doing it since we arrived in town?

I can't do it anymore. I need someone to calm me down a little. I pull out my cell phone and call Simone. Simone answers on the second ring and I go right into the story before she can even get a word out. I tell Simone about Summer and how she was Sean's first love. I tell her about my anxiety about seeing Summer in person and what would happen if she and Sean were alone. I tell her about the first meeting at Natalie's store and the wink.   I tell her about the admission of the kiss. I then tell her about catching Summer on top of Sean less than an hour ago.

"Damn, girl. What you going to do?" Simone asks when I finish giving her the rundown.

"I'm coming home. I'm going to move my stuff out of the Condo and I guess

I'm sleeping in your guest bedroom until I find me a place."

"Lexis, you know I turned that guest bedroom into my office."

"Well, I'm sleeping on the couch!" I yell.

"Hold on with the tone. And are you sure you're not jumping the gun?" Simone asks.

My voice stays elevated. "He was eating her out on the break room floor. What would you do?"

"Probably kick his ass. But in your case, I would talk to him first because you don't know what really went on."

"Well, he didn't come out to talk to me so I guess he stayed and enjoyed himself."

Simone knows all about my past boyfriends, even the drug dealer who got my little brother locked up. "I'm just saying that I know Sean and he loves you. The way he looks at you tells me that you are the only one he wants to be with. If you ask me, I say something doesn't seem right."

"I guess neither of us knew Sean as well as we thought. In the end, he's just like all the rest. I'm done with men for good. From now on it's just me and God."

"Come on now. You can't stay away from the magic stick anymore than I can," Simone says.

"Watch me. I'm going to be celibate for
the rest of my life." I even had to laugh
a little at my declaration.
Simone laughed a little as well. "All I'm
saying, Cuz, is talk to him first. Sean's
a good man. You don't want to lose
that. Do you?"
"He got his ring back. Enough said," I
tell her as I finish packing the suitcase.
"Well if that's what you want, Cuz, I
have your back. I just think it's a
mistake," Simone tells me.
"Girl, just pick me up from Bob Hope
International in a few hours. I'll call you
when I land."
"Okay, Lexis."
I hang up with Simone and do a Goggle
search on my phone to find a taxi
service. I find one and make the call to
have one pick me up and take me to the
airport. I place the key on the card
table in the small kitchen area and walk
out of the small apartment locking the
bottom lock on my way out. I walk to
the sidewalk and wait for my taxi, which
should be arriving within fifteen
minutes. I look at my empty ring finger
and begin to tear up again, but I don't
let them fall. I'm done crying. A
cheater like Sean doesn't deserve my
tears. I begin to pray that God help me

get though this heartache and pain I'm
feeling right now.

Chapter 25

Sean

I'm pissed because I was speeding towards the airport trying to catch Alexis before she left for Los Angeles. Then I get a text from Eric that said Krystal was back at Natalie's store and Alexis was at my parents' place packing. He also said Alexis was going to get a taxi to take her to the airport. I get off I 580 East and hop on I 580 West trying to get to my parents' place before Alexis leaves.

I pull in front of my parents' place and see Alexis standing on the curb, still waiting for a taxi. I put the car in park but don't turn off the engine. I hop out and run to her. She tries to back away from me when I try to hug her. I have a chance to make this right and I'm not going to waste it.

"Sean, I don't want to talk to you," she says trying to avoid eye contact with me. "Baby, you have to believe me. I didn't do anything wrong."

Alexis finally looks me in the eyes. I see the rage in hers. Before I can do or say anything else, she slaps me across the face.

"You didn't do anything wrong? You had a naked woman on your face!" Alexis yells as tears form in her already red and puffy eyes.

"I was set up, Alexis. From the very beginning I was set up."

I figured it all out when I saw Eric's text message from Summer. Summer had it planned from the beginning. She called me the other night because she knew I would be intrigued by her needing to talk to me. She knew that if she seemed hurt at the mall yesterday, that I would try and make it right by coming to her house and finishing our talk. She knew that I would stop her this morning and she made sure she dropped me off in front of Alexis where everyone could see. She took Alexis' phone and text me to meet her in the dressing room and then got me caught up in what seemed like us having sex. Summer always gets what she wants, but I've never seen her go to such extraordinary measures to do so.

"Men are always set up when they get caught doing wrong" Alexis says as her taxi pulls in front of the house and parks. She walks past me to the taxi driver, who has gotten out of the car. He takes her suitcase and puts it in the trunk. "I'll leave the key to the condo under the mat."

I run to Alexis and stop her from getting into the taxi. She tries to wrestle out my grip, but I'm too strong for her. She bites my hand which makes me release one hand. She then slaps me again and starts hitting me in my face, arms and chest. I grab her arms and restrain her. The taxi driver comes towards me to intervene. I give him a look that makes him back down. He gets into his cab and gets on the phone, probably calling the police.

"Alexis just listen to me."

"No!" She screams still trying to get away from me.

"She lied to Eric this morning."

Alexis finally stops trying to fight me seeing she can't win.

"Baby, she set me up from the beginning."

I tell Alexis about the text Summer sent to Eric this morning and how I got a text

to meet her, not Summer, in the
dressing room. Alexis doesn't believe
me at first, but I tell her to look at her
phone. She pulls out her phone, but
there is no text sent to me in her
history. She tries again to get into the
taxi. I hold her with one arm and pull
out my cell phone and show her the text
requesting that I come to the break
room. Reading the text, Alexis sees that
the text is from her phone.
Alexis goes from hurt to furious. "I'm
going to kick her ass! No, I'm going to
kill her!"☐"No need, Baby. I'm still here
with you. You're the one I want to be
with."
"But she was on top of you and you
were... You had your face in her...."
I tell Alexis the whole story and how I
tripped and before I could get up
Summer was on top of me. I told her
how Summer got up after she walked
and in and saw us. I tell her that
Summer just wanted to have sex with
me and that hopefully it would make me
fall in love with her again. I told
Summer it was too late and that I only
wanted to be with her.
Alexis smiles and kisses me. "I'm sorry,
I shouldn't have hit you."
"It's okay. I just want us to be alright."

"If you're willing to give me my ring back then we will be."

"Only if you promise not to take it off again."

Alexis kisses me again. "I promise."

I take the ring out of my pants pocket and place it back on her finger. I kiss her and hug her tight. I tell the taxi driver to take the suitcase out of the trunk and have him call off the police. He tells me he didn't call the cops. He called his wife to check on the kids. He says this wasn't the first time he's seen a couple fight. I give him thirty bucks and he drives off. Alexis and I stand on the curb. I hug her and kiss her again, happy that I didn't lose her.

"So does this mean she's truly out of your system?" Alexis asks.

I nod. "Summer is out of my system for good. You don't have to worry about Summer ever again."

Epilogue

Summer

I sit in the back of Fellowship Baptist
Church. I arrived late to the church
Anniversary service and had gone
unnoticed by everyone. It is packed
with members of other churches in
attendance. I wasn't as worried about
the service as I was about the outcome
of my plan to get Sean. I expected
Alexis to leave town last night and Sean
would run to me for comfort, but it
never happened.
I listened to the end of Reverend
Winters' sermon on forgiveness. Sean
called me last night and apologized for
how he talked to me at Natalie's store. I
thought it was the opening to him
professing his love, but instead he told
me he only wanted to be with Alexis. I
was crushed but didn't feel defeated.
After a few drinks, I renewed my faith to

make Sean mine. I just need Alexis out of the way. She doesn't deserve him. Alexis can't love Sean the way I do and soon he'll find out she's not the one for him.

Reverend Winters made a special announcement that Sean was engaged. Everyone clapped expect me. Sean and Alexis stand and wave to everyone, full of smiles. Reverend Winters goes on to announce that Sean would help re-build the church and bring it back to life. This brought more applause. Sean already put up twenty thousand dollars for remodeling. Reverend Winters also says that Sean will be raising more money in the coming months.

The next announcement is about Andrea, who is set to start school at San Francisco State and double majoring in Dance and Business. This brought even more applause as Andrea, who is seated in the front row with her mother stands and waves. I find it odd that the Winters family seems so happy so soon. I know all about Sean and Reverend Winters dislike for each other. And since when did Reverend Winters become a man that sends his daughter to dancing school? It's just not his style.

I start to think about how I'll get Sean
back. The only problem is Alexis. I
need to find a way to make Sean see
that Alexis isn't the perfect little woman.
The problem is that she seems like the
perfect woman. But everyone has
something; everyone has skeletons in
their closet. I am going to find Alexis'
deep, dark secret. There has to be
some dirt on Alexis out there and I'm
going to be the one to expose it. By the
time I'm done, Alexis will regret the day
she stepped foot in Sean's studio and
stole him from me. Alexis doesn't know
who the hell she just pissed off.
Summer Boyd wasn't the one to play
with. Alexis just started a war of the
hearts. She may have won this battle,
but she won't win the war.
The service ends and people exit the
sanctuary. I get up first and walk out
trying to avoid being seen. I quickly
walk through the lobby and towards the
exit door. A church member who knows
my mother stops me. We make small
talk for a moment. As the woman says
goodbye, I look to the lobby and make
eye contact with Alexis who is standing
with Sean, but he is looking in the
opposite direction. Alexis' smiling face
turns to a frown as she stares at me. I

smile and wink at her then exit the church.

I walk to my BMW and get in. I check my make-up in the visor mirror. I smile at my reflection, thinking to myself, "How can Sean not want me?" My first plan to get Sean back failed, but I always get what I want. I don't know the date for Sean's wedding, but I plan for them not to make it to the alter. Sean is mine and no little model is going to take him away from me. He is just confused right now and Alexis has him not thinking straight. She's got him brain washed.

"So what is my next move?" Whatever it is it has to be big so that Sean knows that I really want to be with him and only him. I think about a question my little sister, Nicole, asked me a few years back. "What do you do when the one you love doesn't love you back?" My answer was, "Make them love you." And that's what I plan to do. I am going to make Sean love me.

Disclaimer

The church used in this novel is a work
of fiction. Though there is a church on
the corner of 44th Street and Linden in
North Oakland it is not the church in
this novel. Also the homes of The Good
Reverend Winters, Summer's parents'
and Summer's condo, Sean's studio and
condo are all fictitious. Natalie's store is
also a work of fiction.

Book Club Questions

1. Do you believe Sean made the right choice in staying with Alexis?
2. What could Summer have done differently to get Sean back?
3. Do believe Sean cheated on Alexis when he kissed Summer?
4. Is having an emotional love affair worse than having a physical affair?
5. Do you think Sean still loves Summer?
6. Do you believe Summer really loved Sean?
7. Should Alexis have told Sean to confront his feelings for Summer?
8. Do you believe Alexis is a hypocrite because off of her profession? She loves God, but she poses half naked is magazines and videos. Even though it's stated her work is tasteful, is she sending a bad message to young Christian women?

9. Do you believe that Sean was ever in control with his relationship with Summer?

10. Do you believe Sean was wrong for holding a grudge against The Good Reverend Winters for his past infidelity?

11. Do you believe The Good Reverend Winters deserved forgiveness from Sean? From Toni? From his congregation?

12. Would you take care of you husbands out-of-wedlock child?

13. Do you believe Toni to be weak strong?

14. What are the similarities between Alexis and Summer? What are their differences?

15. What is Sean's attraction Summer? To Alexis?

Acknowledgements

I thank God forgiving me the gift of
writing. I thank God for giving me the
idea of Winters' Summer as I flew home
from a visit to LA ten years ago. I thank
God for guiding me on this journey of
life. I have been blessed beyond what I
deserve.

If you have not yet accepted Jesus as
your personal Lord and Savior I urge
you to do so. I am not a perfect man
nor do I pretend to be. What I am is a
sinner saved by grace. Grace and mercy
are free gifts from God. For God so
loved the world that He sent His only
begotten son Jesus to die for the worlds
sins John 3:16. We didn't do anything
to deserve it. All we have to do is accept
it. To me it's simple. Accept the free gift
of Grace and have eternal life in heaven.
I have my ticket to Glory I urge you to
get yours.

To my wife Nasinet (Nasa) I love you so
much. I appreciate you for always

having my back and supporting me.
Thank you for taking the kids out of the
house and giving me hours to focus on
my writing. Thank you for being my
toughest critic and my best friend. I
LOVE YOU.
I thank my kids Bryan and Menah
because you guys taught me patience
and helped me to stop procrastinating
and making excuses for why I'm not
writing. You don't know it but you two
made me grow up and get my priorities
straight.
I thank my parents Ellis and Stephanie
Jackson. My parents are the most
supportive parents in the world. I love
you guys. You have banked rolled all of
my projects so this book is as much
yours as it's mine.
I thank my brother Marcus Jackson for
always showing support. If it wasn't
mom and dad you were bank rolling me
and I appreciate it.
I thank my grandmother Helen Woods
who helped raise and shape me. I love
you.
I want to thank my editors/proofreaders
and cousins Ronald Jackson II and
Douita Woods. You helped mold this
manuscript into a great story.
I have to thank all my Uncles, Aunts
and Cousins who have supported me

over the years. Here goes and I pray I hope don't forget anybody: Uncle Ron and Auntie Jan, Uncle Rick and Auntie Ella, Auntie Kathy and Uncle Clyde, Uncle Ken, Jason, Chelia, Brigee, Shavaki, Andre, Theresa (French Fri.), Kim Richardson, Hana Coleman, Danielle, Asokah, Auntie Bette, Aunt Lynn, Shonda, Charles Jackson and Norma, Charles (LA), Carlos, Bobbie, Carmen, Bonnie, Cookie, Exzetta, Art, Eric and Ron, Donnie, and Jessica. If I missed anyone charge it to my head and not my heart.

I want to thank my friends and supporters: Tyjun, Antrina, Ben, Valerie Patton, Arthur Young, Christina and Mike Glendinning, Kay-c, De Young, Mieko, Joy Morgan, Darrin Hodges, Darrin and Lori Baker, James and Loni Battle, Joan Leadbetter, Diana and Steve McCarter, Denise Tracy, Dave Gregory, Angel, Jahi and Lori, Terrence (K. C.), Lisa Luttinger, Jovan and Kelly (Nikki B).

Special thanks to David and Lyn Talbert. David, you told me to keep writing and I haven't stopped since. Special thanks to Mary "Honey B" Morrison. You have given me priceless advice. I appreciate it.

Special thanks to authors Kimberla
Lawson Roby and Lutisha Lovely. I
haven't met you in person but our e-
mails have given lots of advice.

I want to thank all of my co-workers at
the Kaiser Permanente Optical Lab who
came out to my plays and have
supported me in my writing career.
Especially everyone in the
administration office who kept
encouraging me to keep writing.

I want to give special thanks to Pastor
Donel Reedus, First Lady Judy Reedus
and the entire East Bay Bible Church
family. I love you all and appreciate all
of the support over the years. If you're
looking for a church home please visit
eastbaybiblechurch.com. Also check us
out on the radio KFAX 1100-AM
Sundays at 3 pm. Yes, that was a
commercial.

I also want to thank Pastor Allen Barns
and the Community Baptist Church
family. Community is where I first
accepted Jesus as my Lord and Savior.
Though I don't get to see the members
much I want you to know there is no
loss of love or respect for my original
church family.

I also want to acknowledge those who
are no longer here but left me with
words of wisdom. May you rest in

peace. Ellis Jackson (Grandpa Jack),
Henry Woods (Grandpa Woody), Ruth
Mary Jackson (Grandma Ruth), Barbra
Bailey, Uncle Earl, Aunt Georgia Lee
Sexton, Aunt Stella and Aunt Ruby.

Coming Soon!!!!

Sonny Knights

About the Author

D. Lamar Jackson was born and raised in Oakland, California. He is a graduate of San Francisco State University. He has written several stage plays as well as the novella Lilies in Spring. He is the editor and chief of D. Lamar Ink, llc. Winters' Summer is the first novel under this imprint. The next novel Sonny Knights is scheduled for a 2013 release. D. Lamar still resides in the Bay Area with his wife and two children. For all news, info and updates visit www.dlamarink.com or follow him on Twitter @dlamarthewriter or on Facebook under the handle D. Lamar Jackson.

333

www.ingramcontent.com/pod-product-compliance
Lightning Source LLC
Chambersburg PA
CBHW051234260626
47162CB00002B/426